## *Feel the Bu...*

The whole idea began to sound appealing. An exercise video *for* today's typical teens like me, *by* typical teens like me. So what would that look like, exactly?

I saw designer fashions.

I saw taut teen bodies warming up in unison.

I saw soft, affirmative lighting.

I heard music—not Jurassic rock or complaint rock, but today's totally chronic pump-up rock.

I saw an entire world of couch potatoesque teens being guided to flab-freeing fitness by me. The far-reaching makeover possibilities made me feel warm and fuzzy all over.

And then I saw the most furiously golden sight of all. I was not alone! My friends were demonstrating alongside me, teaching all of teenage America the most radical moves to Bettyville. The video was for teens. As in all of us together. Team video. And the mother of all makeover projects!

**Other Clueless™ books**

CLUELESS™
A novel by H. B. Gilmour
Based on the film written and directed by Amy Heckerling

CLUELESS™: CHER'S GUIDE TO . . . WHATEVER
By H. B. Gilmour

CLUELESS™: ACHIEVING PERSONAL PERFECTION
By H. B. Gilmour

CLUELESS™: AN AMERICAN BETTY IN PARIS
By Randi Reisfeld

CLUELESS™: CHER NEGOTIATES NEW YORK
By Jennifer Baker

Available from ARCHWAY Paperbacks

# Cher's Furiously Fit Workout

Randi Reisfeld

AN ARCHWAY PAPERBACK
Published by POCKET BOOKS
New York London Toronto Sydney Tokyo Singapore

AN ARCHWAY PAPERBACK *Original*

An Archway Paperback published by
POCKET BOOKS, a division of Simon & Schuster Inc.
1230 Avenue of the Americas, New York, NY 10020



ISBN: 0-671-00322-4

First Archway Paperback printing October 1996

10 9 8 7 6 5 4 3 2 1



Printed in the U.S.A.

IL: 7+

## Acknowledgments

I *have* to be honest.

Way major props go to my righteous homegirls, Fran Lebowitz of Writer's House for her support and encouragement and Anne Greenberg of Pocket Books, for, like, the same thing.

And okay, so then there are the usual random generics who said stuff like "This doesn't make any sense at all" and "This is funny?" and "I don't really have time to read this, but I'm sure it's fine," etc., etc., and all that other way helpful stuff.

A rampant merci beaucoup to computer doc Mike Mandelbaum, who said, "Are you mentally challenged or what? Your computer didn't crash. Just divide the book into different documents, and that box that says 'Does not have enough memory to continue the operation' will be gone." Like, whew!

And great big wet sloppy kisses to Marvin, Scott, Stefanie, and yes, there really is a Peabo. Like always. With love. Totally.

# Cher's Furiously Fit Workout

# Chapter 1

The Beverly Hills boutique branch of the California Pizza Kitchen was way aggravated with wall-to-wall randoms waiting to get in. "Did you let them know we were coming, Cher?" my best friend De turned to me and asked impatiently.

"Tscha! Totally covered, girlfriend." I smiled and patted my cellular. "You'll be gnashing those million-dollar incisors into your first fat-free slice"—I consulted my gold Movado—"in ten."

As if on cue, a maitre d' elbowed his way through the crowd and approached. "Ms. Cher Horowitz!" he said, beaming in that truly sincere faux Beverly Hills fashion. "I see you and your party"— he turned to acknowledge De and my other friend, Tai—"have arrived. Your table is waiting. Allow me to escort you." With that, he turned and led us to our regular corner booth tucked safely away from the hoi polloi, deep in the VIP section.

Like how typical is this scene. Me, De, and Tai wrapping our traditional Tuesday après-school buying and bonding spree with a blitz blast at one of our regulars, CPK.

Even though we're teenagers, we're not the angst-filled kind so often represented in the media. Like, *hello?* Why would we be? We're in the prime hottie years of our lives. We've got flawless figures on which hang only the most golden designer fashions. Boys fall all over themselves to even pretend they know us. Just like in the Mentos commercials, we take every life situation and put our own cool spin on it. We are totally the bomb.

Of course, we do have that little annoyance known as high school to contend with. But even in those hallowed halls, we're majorly revered by the entire cast and crew of peer group, teachers, and administrators alike. Life is, essentially, fabulous. Like the shiny Gucci hip-huggers nesting comfortably in the gold-and-white-striped shopping bag at my knees.

Best of all, I thought, surveying my t.b.'s sitting across from me, we've got one another.

"I'll have the grilled eggplant cheeseless pizza, with the salt-free sauce, leave off the sun-dried tomatoes and slice the olives really thin." De was dictating precisely. She'd lowered her Cazale sunglasses onto the bridge of her nose and batted her long dark eyelashes, focusing intently on the waiter. She wasn't flirting—it was just rampantly important that he got the order right. De had her priorities straight. That's one of the things that drew us together, back when we first met. Which is the stuff that becomes a legend fast. Or most. Whatever.

I'm a Caucasian-American princess with swingy, shiny blond hair and a designer wardrobe to die for. De's African-American teenage royalty with hazel eyes, and a sharp-tongued wit to die from. We bonded immediately, instinctively aware of being the envy of the entire population. And then we found we had so much more in common. Like, we were both named for celebrity dudettes of the past who now hawk medieval clothes catalogues or communicate with their psychic friends. Together, De and I set the standard the rest of the school strives for.

"And for you?" The waiter turned his cheesy gaze at Tai. She gave him her rendition of flirting.

"Uhmb, uh, I'll do the Thai chicken personal pie," she said. "It's my namesake pizza." As if the waiter was remotely interested. Before Tai could further humiliate herself, I jumped in cheerily. "And I'll just do the tre-color salad—arugula, endive, radicchio, no-oil dressing on the side," I said automatically, flashing a blinding smile in his direction.

Saving Tai from herself had become second nature to me. Originally, De and I had taken Tai on as a project. Before meeting us, her hair was a jungle of knots, and her of idea of fashion was whatever had fallen next to her bed the night before. Tai was so adorably clueless, we just had to help. With coaching, no-more-tangles Tai had achieved her personal best and was very nearly a Betty like us. But she was still tripping all over herself in the social graces aisle of the boutique of life.

Totally pleased with myself for rescuing Tai from foot-in-mouth syndrome, I was reveling in my homeostatic—PSAT word, pretty groovy, huh?—moment when I was brutally interrupted by a cacophonous jangle of jewelry, worn by—

"Hi, guys—sorry I'm late. Slide over for me? I'm only a size two, so I don't need much room."

Size two? As if! The fashion disaster victim that was Amber Salk had suddenly and impertinently invaded our space. Worse, she was acting as if someone had, like, invited her. What's up with that? I looked at De, who shrugged her shoulders, indicating she wasn't the perp. So that left . . .

"Oh, hi, Amber," mumbled Tai. "Sure, sit down. There's room next to Cher. Right, Cher?" Tai's mea culpa look was brutally obvious. Still, I slid over without asking Tai what alien invaded her cloud-puff brain and forced her to invite Amber, who grates on me like an officious saleswoman at Saks.

Okay, so in some ways, Amber is one of us. But fashion is so not one of those ways. Take today. While we were attired in school-appropriate Chanel and DKNY, she was all Malibu Barbie, halter top and leopard print mini-skirt, accessorized with bracelets, bangles, and her version of a Y necklace.

I was so busy being astounded by Amber's ensemble, I was totally not tuned in to the table talk. When I clicked in, Tai was reading something, and De was talking.

"You know that part in the movie where Angela set

the car on fire?" De was saying. She had a faraway look in her eyes, and her fork, on which she'd speared an olive, was in midair. "I think that's my favorite part. It so captures a woman's fiery rage," she finished dramatically, exhaling deeply while inhaling the olive.

Ever since snagging the video *Waiting to Exhale,* De kept coming up with favorite parts. So far I'd counted seventeen. Personally? I didn't think the movie was deserving of such intense, daily dissection. Okay, so it had the sisterhood-affirmation thing happening, but once you'd seen it, it was, doy, *over.* The women booted the men, bonded, and everyone sang. Roll the credits.

But De seemed chronically affected. Or infected.

"You know, I've never really explored this side of my heritage before," she was saying thoughtfully. Which always signaled trouble. Thoughtfully wasn't one of De's major manners of speaking.

"I mean, here I am this perfect African-American Jewish princess who only knows one side of herself. It's so incomplete. It's like an entire Versace sheath without the beaded jacket. You know what I mean?"

Okay, so she'd come up with an analogy even I got.

"Maybe it's time to get in touch with my inner African-American princess," De continued, "explore my roots. Murray's always on me for that."

Murray was De's significant other. As in boyfriend. They'd hooked up in junior high school, but still hadn't gotten their love-vehicle out of second gear. They were forever stalled at the intersection of Dysfunction Junction and Lip-Lock Lane. Walking out or making up. Either way, it was way dramatic.

At school, Murray's part of the Crew, the boy zone encompassing the only acceptable choices if you had to date a high school boy. My personal choice in the matter is, as if! High school boys are like amoebas with droopy pants and backward baseball caps. A flotilla of single-celled, single-minded fashion flops. Personally, I'm looking for a life form just a little higher in the food chain.

"So what do you think, Tai?" I said, hoping to draw a neutral third party into the De-roots discussion. Only this party was off in her own orbit. Crunching loudly on a crusty morsel, Tai's eyes were riveted to what appeared to be a brochure. And since it didn't have Kate Moss or Marvin the Martian on the cover, I couldn't figure the attraction.

"This is such a cool idea," Tai was saying, between noisy, indelicate bites.

"So you like, agree. De should delve into her genetic ancestry?" I asked, surprised.

"De? What ancestry?" Tai looked up for the first time. "No, I was talking about this. Puppy Love," she said, brandishing her brochure in our faces.

"What's that? A dating service for the hydrant-peeing set?" De, who'd finally exhaled, giggled.

Tai either didn't get the joke or chose to ignore it. "No, Puppy Love is an organization that recruits families to train seeing eye dogs for the blind."

De and I and even Amber looked at her blankly.

"See, blind people need seeing eye dogs, right? But they can't train them themselves 'cause if they could, they wouldn't be blind!" Stating the obvious, that's our

Tai. "So volunteer families take these cute little pups, give them a loving home so they'll be comfortable and trusting around people, and teach them commands to help the blind. Then, after a year of training, you give them up to a blind person."

"Very noble. And what this would have to do with you is . . . ?" I asked.

"Tscha! Cher, I'm going to do it."

"Do what? And why?" De, clearly confused, chimed in.

"I got the idea from Dr. Albright, my guidance counselor. He suggested I might need something to balance my transcript."

Academia alert. Tai's study skills needed an immediate upgrade. But before I could whip out my Granello appointment book to make a grade-improvement date, Tai was all, "So we went through all these community service type ideas, and came up with this brochure for Puppy Love. And I don't know, it sounded so . . . right."

"Sounds like an undertaking of humongous proportions," I said, going for the diplomatic.

"Sounds messy," De said, turning her nose up.

Amber took it upon herself to be the tie breaker. "Well, if you want my opinion . . ."

Before I could make it plain that, like, thanks, but no thanks, she cleared her throat and announced, "I agree with Dr. Albright. You do need something that looks positive on your transcript, Tai."

"While *you* need something that looks positive on your body," I pointed out.

Amber turned to me and said, "I'm sorry if you don't agree, Cher. But I *have* to be honest. Tai's grades are anemic. Community service always looks good."

I might have gone on sparring with Amber, but Tai had tuned us both out. "It's the best feeling, you guys, helping humanity and all," she said dreamily. "You should think about it, Cher. After all, helping is so part of you."

"Not even!" I countered. "The only canines that are part of me have Gund tags around their necks."

As we flashed plastic to cover the bill, I wondered how this perfect bonding afternoon had come unglued so quickly. I mean, it should have been the most monster day. But before I'd gotten two sentences out about our Galleria plans for tomorrow, De was all, "Count me out, Cher. I'm going over to the Waldenbooks at the Beverly Center. I've gotta do this. I'm stocking up on Toni Morrison, Maya Angelou, and that Oprah cookbook thing. Catch you later."

Tai was similarly—and uncharacteristically—unwilling to commit. "Gotta go over to Puppy Love headquarters. I'll beep you when I'm done."

And then there was Amber. The question, Why? lingered.

# Chapter 2

Without getting my fingernails dirty—metaphorically speaking, that is—I was still trying to unearth the roots of my general feeling of ickiness when I got home. Usually, just walking up our cobblestoned circular driveway lifts my spirits. But even that wasn't working today. I live in a furiously fabulous multistoried mansionette, accessorized with columns and balconies. Out front is a monster lawn, and out back, an Olympic-size pool, tennis courts, and riotously color-coordinated garden. It's totally high maintenance, but that's what gardeners and household staffs are for.

I live here with Daddy, my sole parental unit. He's a litigator, which is sort of like a legal alligator, only with fewer swamps and sharper teeth. Just saying his name is enough to inspire fear and trepidation over each and every manicured hill of Beverly. Sometimes I think I'm the only one who isn't afraid of Daddy. Like, hello? Why would I be? He and I have a way evolved relationship. Although we usually avoid discussing matters of a personal nature, he totally relies on me for his nutritional and sartorial needs. And in the ultimate sense—plastics—he totally takes care of me.

Today, however, I wasn't really up for an interface. So I was less than thrilled when, as soon as I got through the door, I heard Daddy calling from his office.

"Cher! Good. You're home. Come in here. I have some people for you to meet."

"Less than thrilled" morphed into "severely unthrilled" when I saw who was in Daddy's office. There were three people, but I barely noticed two of them. Directly in front of Daddy's desk, however, stood the alterna-stepbrother himself. In the flannel.

Josh would have been the bane of my incredibly perfect existence, except he wasn't around enough to qualify. Our history was mercifully brief. His mother, Gail-the-galloping-neurotic, had her mani-claws in Daddy ever so fleetingly. In other words, they'd been married. That, however, is so ancient history, and when Gail returned to her natural habitat—Portland—Josh went with her. Except for the occasional cameo, he was mostly absent from our lives. Which worked for me.

Daddy had the speaker phone on, a cellular in his hand, and two other lines blinking, but he made the introductions. "Boys, this is my daughter, Cher." Two identical law-clones sitting in a pair of wing chairs nodded in unison in my direction. Then Daddy barked into the speaker phone, "You call that a settlement? I call it an insult! Don't bother me until you come anywhere near the ballpark or I'll have you tarred, feathered, and disbarred!" Daddy punched the speaker button off and continued with the intros.

"Cher, this is Fred Eichler and Ed O'Malley. They're law students who are going to be around for the next few weeks, helping me on the Zinger deposition." That was the big case Daddy had been working on. Anyway, it's Daddy's policy to bring in tender young lawyers-to-be and train them to be vicious piranhas like him. It's his most unselfish contribution to his profession.

"And look who else is here!" Daddy finished jubilantly as if this were like, a good thing. He motioned unnecessarily at the grunge icon. "Your brother, Josh, came aboard to help, too. He's decided to take some undergraduate pre-law courses at UCLA." Uh-oh, it looks as if Josh's cameo is about to stretch into a recurring guest role.

"He's not my brother. He's not even my stepbrother. We're not related in any way, shape, or form. It's *ex* as in extraneous and totally over." Okay, so I knew that sounded petulant, but this hadn't been my most golden day. And this was so not helping.

"Nice to see you, too, Cher. I see the maturity hormone hasn't kicked in yet, but"—with a nod at my shopping bag—"at least the retailers on Rodeo Drive aren't feeling the pinch yet." Josh was all calm. Which is so like him.

"And I see that taste in clothes hasn't invaded your planet yet either." While Fred and Ed were in their dutiful best-to-impress-Daddy outfits, Josh was all,

"Why bother?" His jeans smacked of the uber-generic Gap, and the shirt was maybe . . . J. Crew? I couldn't take myself there.

"Kids, kids, come on." Daddy actually winked at us. "Ex, schmex, we're family."

I was about to protest that like, so were the Menendezes, when Daddy remembered something. "By the way, how'd you do on that algebra test, Cher?" No matter how busy Daddy is, he never loses his place in matters of my academic life. In fact, he'd zoned in on what was turning out to be the highlight of my day: sophomore algebra.

"Aced it, Daddy. I figured out what all the X's were—and lots of Y's and Z's, too," I said proudly, with a glance at Fred and Ed.

"So I guess that means you got an A?" Daddy asked.

"Totally rhetorical—in the end, anyway."

At Daddy's arched eyebrows, I explained, "My teacher actually tried to gyp me out of my deserved grade. I admit to a couple of inconsequential partial misanswers, but she wasn't giving me full credit for my thought process."

"What were you thinking about, the best route to Giorgio's?" Josh flashed his blazing blue eyes at me. Did he always have that dimple?

Turning away from Josh, I went on, "I explained like, how if the Armani is the X and it only comes in fuchsia, and the burnt orange Alaïa is the Y, but it comes in my size, wasn't that the same as those two trains leaving the station and when would they cross in Milwaukee and all? I mean, the thought process was totally the same. And like, how could I not buy them both at the same price? I totally got the teacher to see my side of it. She had to give me the A then."

"She was probably too stunned to do anything else," Josh couldn't resist saying.

Daddy put the cellular down and came around from behind his mahogany and leather desk to give me a hug. "You got the A, right? I'm proud of you, Cher. You did great."

"I learned from the best, Daddy. You! Speaking of which, the best looks like he could use a nutritional infusion. I'll be right back with a snack," I said in my extreme-cuteness tone, for the benefit of the law-clones. I mean, not that either was remotely my type, but you never know when the benefits of flirting will pay off. I'd noticed a Ferrari in the driveway, which had to belong to one of them. It completely isn't Josh's style. Not that you could use *Josh* and *style* in the same sentence, anyway. And rides in golden wheels are something I often covet, since Daddy has this habit of taking away my driving privileges for the tiniest little infraction. I always keep a stack of back-up drivers in my mental Rolodex.

As I bounced off toward the kitchen, I was feeling massively better, like I always do when Daddy and I are in sync. And in spite of Josh.

I was halfway there when I heard something. What were those noises? It sounded like heavy breathing followed by moaning and groaning. In Swedish? It seemed to be coming from the Great Room. That's our 40′× 50′ white-on-white living space, furnished with the latest in high-end furniture and high-gloss technology—big screen TV, VCR, laser disc player, monster CD system—that no one ever used, mainly because the remote that controlled everything was perennially MIA. Except someone was inhabiting the room now. I rounded the corner and peeked in.

"Lucy?" I could not believe my eyes. I would have rubbed them, except I'd done such a stellar job with my MAC makeup and couldn't chance ruination. Anyway, the mega-myopically challenged couldn't have missed this. Center stage in the Great Room was our housekeeper, Lucy. "What are you doing?" I asked incredulously.

Lucy was on her hands and knees. Make that one knee. She was trying, and failing, to thrust the other one up and to the side and hold it for the count of five. Or something.

"Uh, uh, uh . . . Cher!" Lucy was panting when she swung her head around to face me. "I did not realize you were here. I was taking your advice to get some exercise, but this is hard! How can I follow the tape if I'm bending down and stretching? I can't see it," Lucy complained.

My opinion? Seeing was the least of the problems. Like who could be expected to work out to that music? I've heard of sweatin' to the oldies, but this was like drowning in the moldies. Music to be in a coma by.

And then there was the exercise dudette leading the tape. Like, what could Lucy possibly have in common with Claudia Schiffer?

"Lucy, turn that off, and follow me," I gently instructed, and began demonstrating some low-impact stretches. "You start slowly, warm up first, you know?

It's like preheating the oven before you start to cook." I was proud of myself for coming up with a cooking metaphor—something Lucy could relate to. In fact, they really ought to come up with an exercise video for real housekeepers like Lucy. "Extreme Vacuuming" or something.

"This is better, easier." Lucy looked relieved.

"We'll do more tomorrow, okay? I'm not exactly dressed for working out now. Besides, I promised Daddy I'd get him a snack. Do we have those no-fat rice cakes?"

"The ones your father calls no-taste? Ya, they're on the lower shelf of the pantry."

When I got back to Daddy's office with his snack—a rice cake topped with squiggles of I Can't Believe It's Not Butter and ringed with orange slices, and ginger-peach tea—I noticed the troops du jour, Fred, Ed, and yes! thankfully the detested ex, Josh, had departed.

"What is this, Cher?" Daddy eyed his snack suspiciously. "More of that cardboard tree-trunk garbage you try to camouflage?"

As I set the tray down on his desk, I reminded him, "It's too close to dinner for anything else, Daddy. Besides, with all the stress of the Zinger thingie, you've got to be especially judicious about what you eat. Stress causes a breakdown in your immune system, and the world needs you in top fighting form."

"Stress!" Daddy harumphed. "What a whiny me-generation invention. In my day, who ever heard of stress? We had problems, then we solved them. And we ate whatever we pleased. *That* made us feel better."

I gave Daddy my best persuasive smile. When logic didn't work, it was time for tactic number two: genuine daughterly concern. But I guess I was a bit off with my look, because Daddy did a one-eighty. He got all concerned about me.

"What's the matter, Cher? Something's wrong, I can tell."

"What do you mean, Daddy? I'm aces. What could be wrong?" I said innocently.

"It's too quiet, that's what's wrong!" Daddy thundered. "You've been home for a half hour. Why hasn't your phone been ringing?"

Nailed! That's what makes Daddy such a great lawyer. Nothing gets by him. He's so totally perceptive, incisive—and direct. In the jugular sense. Since there was no way I could fool Daddy, I sat down on the studded leather couch, nabbed the rice cake since he wasn't eating it, sighed, and told him everything.

"It's no biggie, Daddy. It's just, well, this afternoon after our shopping spree and CPK cal-fest? You know, me, De, and Tai?"

Daddy came around from behind his desk and sat down next to me. He nodded and waited for me to continue.

"It just wasn't, I don't know, the same."

"The same as what, Cher? Didn't you girls go shopping? And then to that hang-out you usually go to? And won't I be getting a large bill for all of the above?"

"Okay, so that part was the same. But then after the shopping and all, we usually bond. You know, the girlfriend affirmation thing."

"And that didn't happen this time? Is there a boy involved here?"

"Duh, Daddy, of course not. No *boy* could come between us. This is way worse."

Daddy looked majorly parental. I had no choice but to spill all. I told him how De was going on safari to dig up her roots or something and how Tai was starting a new career as a dog trainer and how Amber had inflicted herself into our booth. And now the silent cellular.

"And nobody would even commit to the Galleria tomorrow!" I sounded more pitiful than I meant to. This is so not me.

Daddy smiled gently and put his arm around me. "I wouldn't worry, Cher. You're talking about your best friends. What do you call them, your TVs?"

"T.b.'s, Daddy—true blues. That's what we used to be anyway."

"Nonsense. You and Dionne are like bagels and lox. You can't have one without the other. And that Tai girl. She seems like the loyal type."

My look told him I wasn't so sure about that.

"Okay, Cher, let's think about this. Without having the evidence in front of me, just on your testimony, I'd say that your friends are growing up a little. Maybe De and Tai are just trying to find their niche in the world. They're exploring."

"What's wrong with the niche we used to have? Isn't being beautiful and envied enough of a niche? It's a perfect fit. And why can't we explore together?" Okay, I was whining here.

Then Daddy got even more thoughtful. "Of course

it's also possible that you, De, and Tai are just growing apart," he said, looking directly into my eyes. "These things happen, Cher, even to the best of friends."

"Blue eye shadow happens, Daddy. But not to us."

As I flounced out of Daddy's office to head upstairs to my room, I paused, as I always do, at the portrait of my mom. It dominates the wall in the marble hallway, near the bottom of the circular staircase. Mom was a rampantly bodacious Betty in her day—even if the cutting-edge fashions back then did unfortunately include disco boots. My mom died when I was a baby. They tell me it was a routine liposuction gone berserk.

I don't dwell on negativity or what might have been. Like they say in Bartlett's Great Quotations, or somewhere, you play the hand that's dealt you. And hello? I can't really complain about my hand. Besides, it's not as if Mom and I don't have a relationship. I like to pretend she's looking down at me from disco heaven, and that between dances she totally thumbs-up my life choices. If I told her about the growing apart thing between me and my t.b.'s, I know she wouldn't have accepted it. As I fully intend not to.

# Chapter 3

I go to Bronson Alcott High School. It's a sprawling, one-story ranch-style edifice sporting columns ringed with faux ivy. Inside, it's riddled with classrooms, lockers, gyms, and offices. So I try to spend as much time as possible outdoors. The Quad, a huge, palm-tree-lined rectangle of manicured, rolling green studded with sculptures, fountains, and benches, is our usual hangout. Of course, there hasn't been much in the way of usual lately.

Take yesterday. I'd persuaded one of Daddy's early-bird law clones—I'm not exactly sure which one—into dropping me off at school. So, okay, like the juniors and seniors mostly drive monster cars, but the Ferrari I pulled up in? Total scene-stealer material. I even made sure Fred-Ed circled the parking lot leisurely, so everyone would have proper time and space to admire.

But the only admirees were the randoms. Everyone else was looking at Dionne. She was dressed in a caftan with colors so blinding, I needed extra-strength Armani sunglasses. And what was that on her head? It looked like the Kremlin interpreted as a hat. De had gone from Winnie the Pooh to Winnie Mandela in one fell swoop. She was powwowing with Murray and some other quasi Crew members when I sashayed up to them.

"De, girlfriend, I'm furiously floored by the headgear," I said, attempting our usual light and witty repartee.

"You like?" she said, oblivious to the ambiguity in my tone. She twirled around, so I could appreciate it from all angles. "It's a traditional African chapeau, but with a nineties spin. It's Gaultier. I ordered a dozen of them from the Joe Casely-Hayford catalogue."

A dozen! I could totally not respond to that. But Murray could.

"Yeah, Cher, get with it. I think my woman looks splendiferous." Murray, his braces shooting off glints of sunlight, was decked out in his usual oversize Hilfiger sweatshirt and draggy baggies. He put a protective arm around De. Which she immediately yanked off.

"I am not your woman, Murray—when is that going to register with you?"

Okay, so like how many times had De said that before? It would have been all, "This has been a recording," except for the way she said it. Her eyes flashed and her tone was way harsh. Like she meant it.

Not that Murray noticed. I wouldn't expect him to.

He's her boyfriend, not her best friend. Only a t.b. would notice a subtlety like that.

"I think De looks ferociously phat!" And in this corner: Murray's newest appendage, Sean, weighed in with a superfluous opinion. Though Sean possessed the basic Baldwinesque requirements to be part of the Crew—muscular bod and chiseled face—individuality was a concept he hadn't quite conquered. Lately he'd been hanging on to Murray like that flip part of the cellular.

Suddenly, a weird feeling came over me. *I* felt like the appendage. "Whatever" was all I could muster. "Beep ya later, De. I'm Audi."

On the way to my first period class, I bumped into Amber. The poster child of fashion disasters did not disappoint. She was wearing black-and-white herring-bone stretch pants, with shoes to mismatch. The least she could do was have her clothes programmed into her computer like I do. All you do is point and click, and poof! mismatches begone.

"Oh, hi, Cher," she said in a tone that reeked of the faux-sincere friendship that we totally did not have. "On your way to Hall's class? Because I'm about to make a *très* important announcement. And I wouldn't want you to miss it."

What announcement? I wondered idly. That she'd finally broken down and hired a fashion consultant? "Whatever," I said as I brushed by. Lingering with Ambu-loser wasn't on today's agenda.

Mr. Hall is our debate teacher. He's diminutive, hair-impaired, near-sighted, and recently married to Miss

Geist, our social studies teacher. And even though Mr. Hall's been known to cop an inflexible attitude with report cards, mostly he's learned the fine art of patience.

"People! People! Settle in, take your seats." Mr. Hall was the type who never gave up. Trying to get our attention. Trying to teach us stuff. *Fruitless* was not a word in his personal thesaurus. He cleared his throat and tried to get on track.

"Now, if you remember, class, yesterday we left off with Janet Hong's fine discourse on the V-chip ratings system for television shows. If I'm not mistaken"—he consulted his notes—"Jesse Fiegenhut should be, er, educating us, on the opposing point of view." He looked up expectantly. "Jesse?"

Jesse, tall, tan, and totally self-absorbed, had his back turned to Mr. Hall. He *was* actually having a debate, but not on his topic and not in front of the class. He and Roger Farmingdale were arguing Oasis versus Bush: which band had more alt.cred vs. alt.tude and which had more staying power. Jesse was way passionate about his point, practically screaming, "Don't you even *know* who my father is?" Jesse had played that tune so many times, he should be getting royalties. By now the entire school knew that Jesse's father was a major record company honcho. Which meant Jesse not only got every important CD before release and for free, he got backstage passes for what he called "the most drivin' concerts." An advantage that made him a legend in his own mind.

"Mr. Fiegenhut!" Mr. Hall raised his voice above the

general din. "Can we have your attention? And your oral?"

Jesse swung around to face Mr. Hall. His indigo blue eyes were way blank. "My oral? Was that due today?" he asked.

"It was, Mr. Fiegenhut. I take it you are unprepared. I'm marking that down in my book."

"Wait, Mr. Hall, I have a good excuse." Jesse raised his hand reflexively.

"And what would that be?"

"Dude, I was out mega late last night, in the trenches, checking out the Goo Goo Dolls at the Forum. You know, when you're in the biz, you gotta do the backstage thing, schmooze the talent. It's unavoidable. Being in the music business requires late hours. In fact, I think I should get extra credit for even showing up here today." Jesse surveyed the room. "Who agrees with me?"

General applause broke out among the class.

Amber's hand shot up before Hall could respond.

Mr. Hall looked exasperated, "Yes, Amber?"

"I have an announcement. And since Jesse won't be speaking, I'd like to take his place at the podium." Without waiting for Hall's okay, Amber bounced up from her seat and strode purposefully to the front of the class.

"As we all know," she began, looking around the classroom to be sure she had everyone's attention, "school elections are coming up." Amber, who'd paused for effect, had gotten off to a poor start. No one knew any such thing.

Undeterred, she educated. "Each class gets to elect a slate of officers to represent them, to have a voice in the school. And today, I, Amber Salk, am officially announcing for sophomore class president."

If Amber thought she'd get, like, applause, or even boos or hisses, she was way mistaken. The Iranians in the back of the room were arguing in their native tongue—a hybrid of Farsi mixed with Rolex. Two beepers had gone off, signaling cellular air time had begun, and our resident slacker, Jackson Doyle, had slunk back to sleep and was snoring noisily.

Amber was unfazed. She continued talking, louder. "Doesn't anyone want to know what my platform is?"

"Platform jellies that went out of style a month ago?" I guessed.

Amber ignored me and went into full pronouncement mode. "Support groups should count as electives. That's my platform."

The class remained unmoved as she continued. "Face it, our school body is more highly evolved than those in other high schools. Our curriculum should reflect our unique needs."

Although her presentation was being wildly ignored, somewhere off in that Amber-land brain of hers, there was a kernel of truth to what she was saying. I had to admit that at least half the student population was involved in one support group or another. They had them for single-parent families; stepfamilies one, two, and three (when a parent had remarried several times); children of compulsive gamblers; children of movie stars; children of TV-movie stars.

". . . and I, Amber Salk, plan to work to change all

that," she was now droning. "I mean, think about it. We get credit for courses that will never have any bearing on our lives. Cooking? Like hello? Who in this school will ever actually be within ten feet of a working oven? And auto repair? As if anyone would attempt to fix his or her own luxury car. We *have* to be honest. This is not our lifestyle, nor will it ever be. We should be credited for the courses that have actual bearing on our lives." Amber was getting way dramatic.

Mr. Hall interrupted. "While I applaud your new-found interest in school politics, I have to ask that you conclude your announcement. Class started twenty minutes ago and we haven't gotten to our lesson yet."

"Of course, Mr. Hall," Amber said sweetly. "I'd just like to say, in conclusion, that, my fellow students, I'd like to ask for your support. Together we can change the world."

Amber's conclusion had the same effect her announcement did: no one responded because no one was listening. As she flounced back to her seat, she stopped at my desk. "I'm especially counting on your support, Cher. After all, we are friends. And friends stick together."

I was about to inquire about the beginnings of our friendship, as I must have been napping during that part, but Amber was already in her seat. At this point in the day, my cellular was usually ringing—De beeping in from her Spanish class or Tai with a fashion question. But my cel remained silent.

As I headed to my next class, I found myself wondering where the support groups were for left-out friends? But then I caught myself. I was sounding suspiciously self-pitying and that is so not my style. I remembered what Daddy said about that niche thing and how maybe De and Tai were off finding another one to fit into. Where did that leave me? Somewhere in the vast chasm between debate class and social studies, with no one on the other end of the cellular. But maybe the answer to my problem was right under my nose—it usually was. Maybe I could find a new niche, right here at school. I brightened at the prospect. I could niche-seek, too.

As I walked through the halls, I looked around and began mentally checking off the possibilities.

Over by the lockers were the girl jocks from the basketball team. Even with platforms, I'm still under the height requirement. And although I'm coordinated, I'm pretty sure my gifts lie elsewhere.

The nerds were clustered by the bulletin board advertising the academic decathlon. While I pride myself on my grades, the fact that I normally have a life beyond academics excludes me from their crowd.

I wasn't ethnically diverse enough for the Farsis, the Pan-Hispanics, African-Americans, Asian-Americans, or even the culturally eclectic, mixed-breed Americans—those who had so many different cultures they formed their own.

I kept looking. The boardies? As if! The only wheels beneath my feet where going to be attached to that loqued-out Jeep in the driveway.

The slackers? Not even!

The student council leaders? How do you spell boring?

The new-age flowerheads? They were searching for

their inner selves; under normal circumstances I was majorly content with my outer one.

So that left, what? The remedial reading/detention crowd?

There didn't seem to be a clique for the totally golden and fabulously connected Bettys. And then it hit me. That's because we *were* the crowd. Me, De, Tai, with occasional cameos by Janet, Summer, and sometimes, though I'm loath to admit it, even Amber. *We* were what made it special. Accent the *were*.

Later, in P.E., I ran into De.

"De! Wait till you hear what Ambu-lame showed up in." I was so psyched to see her, I fell right into our usual routine, barely noticing that she wasn't alone.

"Zup, Cher," De said distractedly. "Hang on a minute." I'd caught her midgiggle with three girls I identified as Essence, Shaniqua, and Shawana.

Like, hello? Shaniqua and Essence? Of the fake hair extensions and cubic zirconium nose studs? Just a few weeks ago, the De I knew wouldn't have glanced at her Cartier to give them the time of day. Now they were all, "I know *exactly* what you mean, sister! I have been there!"

Since I was pretty sure I hadn't been there, I turned and started off toward my locker. The lockers were strewn with sophomore girls in various stages of changing into gym clothes. It was way sweaty. Making my way around the benches and piles of clothes on the floor, I couldn't help noticing how some people are so not in shape. Don't they know how rampantly important that is? I mean, we are the world and all that, representatives of our generation. It's one thing for Lucy to be physically unfit, but high school wanna-Bettys? That totally should not be.

"Cher! Where'd you go?" De, all dressed in her gym clothes, had come looking for me. "I turned around and you were gone."

"You actually noticed? I'm surprised. You were in such a deep philosophical conversation with a troika you wouldn't have looked at sideways a month ago that I didn't think you even realized I was there."

My tone was more sarcastic than I'd meant it to be. And it was not lost on De, who shot back, "What are you going on about? Just because I was hangin' with a sister or two."

"Sister? Doesn't *sister* refer to someone in your, like, stratosphere? If I'm not mistaken, Essence's father is in middle management, Shaniqua lives below Sunset, and didn't Shawana once try to get her Lee press-on nails into Murray? These girls might be one another's sisters, but, girlfriend, they're not yours."

De got all thoughtful. She sat down on the bench next to my locker and looked up at me. Very quietly, she said, "You know, Cher, I was afraid you wouldn't understand."

"What is there to understand, De? You've practically deserted me—and our friendship. What do Shaniqua, Essence, and Shawana have that I don't? Besides a different complexion, that is."

"What they have, Cher, is something I can maybe connect with. A shared history."

"What about *our* history?" I demanded. "We've traipsed malls, traded plastic, shared everything: not only history, but geography, algebra, and English notes. And have I not always stood by you in the Murray-go-round?"

"Murray? What's he got to do with it? Cher, you are not hearing me," De said deliberately. "This is big. This is something I need to do. If you were really a t.b., you'd understand that and support me in this journey."

"I would, De, if it didn't totally exclude me. I think they should have named that movie *Waiting to Exclude.*"

With that, I fastened the last button on my gym shirt and headed out to do one hundred crunches. Somewhere between the twentieth and the fortieth, I left pity city and determined to come up with a plan. Something rampantly fabulous that would bring me, De, and our t.b. clique back together. A plan always made me feel better.

# Chapter 4

Days later, the De-parture thing was still weighing heavily. Like that Helmut Lang wool blazer you put on in the morning, and then it gets all hot and sticky in the afternoon. To wit, I remained chronically planless. When I'm feeling like this, the usual antidote is a shopping sidebar—with De. Since she *was* the problem, that was out of the question. Ditto, a spree with Tai, who was all, "Gotta go home and work with Peabo." Or T-Bone. Or Peabrain. Or whatever she'd named the training pup. It had totally jumped to the head of her priorities. I briefly considered asking Amber to accompany me, but sanity returned before I got the phone out of my backpack. Besides, Ambular had actually gotten a committee together to support her candidacy. They were busy making posters and flyers and scheduling debates.

The only stress-reduction choice left was to make emergency appointments with my aromatherapist, reflexologist, manicurist, and colorist. It was Fabianne, my masseuse-on-call, who picked up on my uber-tension.

"Cher, you haven't been this knotted up since the last time you maxed out all your credit cards simultaneously," Fabianne noted as she bore down judiciously on my shoulders. "I just got the kinks out two days ago, and you're as tense as ever. So what's the crisis du jour?"

"Nothing a good plan won't solve," I said, exhaling deeply.

"But you don't have one?" she guessed as she expertly dug her warm, oily fingers into my backbone.

"Not yet," I admitted.

Fabianne was furiously working my lower back when she casually mentioned, "What about exercise?"

"What about it?"

"Well, are you getting enough of the right kind? You know, exercise works wonders on stress."

I considered. Maybe Fabianne was right. Everything I'd been doing so far *was* rampantly passive. Everything I'd been doing, in fact, was being done to me. Maybe that's why nothing had worked and a plan hadn't formulated. Maybe what I needed was a personal trainer.

"What exactly *are* you doing for exercise?" Fabianne was asking. "And don't tell me shopping, because that doesn't count."

Ever since I'd done a few stretches with Lucy, the

truth was, I hadn't been doing any. Not in the abs-of-steel sense.

"Well, there are some exercise tapes in our library, but . . ." I trailed off, thinking about Lucy and that fitness debacle. "None of them really apply to me."

"Fitness tapes aren't supposed to apply to you personally, Cher. They're generic instructional guides to get people started."

"Generic! That's just the problem. What I mean is," I explained, "they should have something like designer workouts. For my niche, for real typical teens like me."

"Well, why don't you create one?" Fabianne suggested offhandedly.

"Create what?"

"Exactly what you just said, Cher—a fitness tape for typical teenagers like yourself. I think that's a superb idea, and you know?"—Fabianne's thumbs were working more deeply than ever before—"It's probably very marketable."

"A fitness tape? Oh, doy. Why don't I just create my own nuclear missile while I'm at it? I mean, how would I? I agree that I'm inventive, resourceful, and clever, but that's way out of my sphere of expertise. No, I think I'll go with the personal trainer idea."

But Fabianne was on a roll. "Hold on a minute, Cher. Maybe this isn't so farfetched. I have an idea. I actually know someone who might be perfect for you."

"I'm not looking for a boyfriend," I quipped, hoping to get Fabianne offtrack.

"No, I mean, he's a personal trainer, and he's had some experience in putting together fitness videos.

The more I think about it, you really ought to meet Buff Bobby."

"Uhm, can we just think about the rest of my massage, Fabianne? I need to relax and soon enough the answer to my problems will appear."

"Just listen to me, Cher."

Duh, what choice did I have? Fabianne was getting ready to envelop me in a seaweed body wrap. I was captive. So I listened.

"Bobby Van Hoosen—everyone calls him Buff Bobby—is a fast-tracker. He's only in his twenties, but he's hot. Everyone's talking about him, suits and celebrities, too. And it's not just hype. He's really good. I went to some of his classes and they really helped." Fabianne had thumbs of steel for sure.

"I heard that he worked behind the scenes on videos with Tamilee Webb and Denise Austin," she continued. "He seems to be in demand. I asked him why he wasn't doing his own videos. He's got the talent, the know-how, and he's camera-friendly, if you know what I mean. He said he really does want to do a video, but he's looking for a hook, something new and different that hasn't been done to death already. Which is why you two might be perfect for each other."

In listening to Fabianne's description of the fabulous Buff Bobby, I wondered if maybe she had a thing for him. Like, why else was she pushing this idea? What was in it for her? But I discarded the self-interest angle. After all, she's been my masseuse for ages and no doubt has my best interests at heart.

"Why don't you meet with him?" Fabianne was saying. "At the very least, maybe he can give you some exercise tips that apply to you. I'll set it up. You never know what might develop. What do you say, Cher?"

"I don't know, Fabianne, I know you're just being righteous and all—"

"Just think about it, Cher. I won't do anything until you give me the go-ahead."

I did think about it. Mainly because I had little else to occupy my rampaging brain cells as, later that night, I lay wide-eyed on my Lauren sheets. A few hours later, the whole idea even began to sound appealing. An exercise video *for* today's typical teens like me, *by* typical teens like me.

So what would that look like, exactly?

I saw designer fashions. Armani Abs-wear? Perfectly Fit Prada? The Vera Wang Workout collection? I couldn't be sure.

I saw taut teen bodies warming up in unison.

I saw soft, affirmative lighting.

I heard music—not Jurassic rock or complaint rock, but today's totally chronic pump-up rock.

I saw an entire world of couch potatoesque teens, like those girls in the lockers, being guided to flab-freeing fitness by me! The far-reaching makeover possibilities made me feel warm and fuzzy all over.

Naturally, I saw myself, front and center, in full-throttle hottie mode, demonstrating the moves.

And then I saw . . . Wait a minute! Hit the Pause button and freeze that frame. Hello? I saw . . . yes! The most furiously golden sight of all. I was not alone!

I saw my friends, De, Tai, Murray, even Sean and Amber, demonstrating alongside me, teaching all of teenage America the most radical moves to Bettyville. The video was for teens, by teens. Plural. As in, all of us together. Team video. And the mother of all makeover projects!

Maybe this *was* it, the niche Daddy was talking about, the one that all of us would fit into. Maybe the freeway back to t.b.-town was strewn with thigh-stretches and ab-crunches. Or something.

Early the next day, I called Fabianne and told her all systems were go for the tête-à-tête with the exercise dude, whatever his name was. A half hour later, I heard a joyful noise, the ringing of my cellular.

"Zup, girlfriend?" I'd gone straight into old t.b. mode without even thinking. The voice on the other end laughed. In a deep, distinctly male sense.

"Well, I'm not your girlfriend. But I hope you're not disappointed. This is Bobby Van Hoosen. Fabianne gave me this number. This is Cher, right?"

"In the exercise-friendly flesh!" I went for adorable, which usually worked as a cover-up for goof-in-mouth syndrome.

Although he didn't respond to my cute, Bobby was charmed already, I could tell. "Fabianne mentioned that you might be interested in doing an exercise video? Something that would appeal to teenagers. That sound right?"

"Not right. Not left. It's dead-on center," I quipped. The silence that greeted me announced that my attempt at a joke had like, ready, aim, oops, misfired. "I meant, yes, absolutely. I'm totally interested."

"Well, then, I'm your man. Let's take a meeting tomorrow at Zuma Sushi to talk about it. Around four, four-thirty sound doable?"

I agreed to the meeting. Now I just needed someone to go with. Much as I trusted Fabianne's recommendation, I could just picture Daddy finding out I went to meet a strange man by myself. I'd be toast.

I called De. "Girlfriend!" I practically burbled into the cellular. "I know you've been, uh, on your journey and all, but I've got this chronic idea and—"

"Could you hold on a minute, Cher? I'm being beeped."

De put me on hold? Okay, I will ignore that and wait patiently. When she came back on the line, I got straight to the point.

"I need you to go with me somewhere." Before De could put me on hold again, I explained all about Buff Bobby, the video, and tomorrow's meeting. "And I was thinking, maybe Murray could drive us?" I finished hopefully. It's not that I couldn't drive myself, but for distances outside of Beverly Hills, I thought it prudent for an actual licensed driver to be at the wheel.

De was all, "What's goin' on, Cher? When did all this happen?"

"When you were all tangled up your roots," I wanted to say, but exercised major sarcasm-restraint. Instead, I kept up the bubbly tone. "Just now! You know how when inspiration hits, you don't ask questions, you just seize the dress. I'm so totally inspired. I need to, what's that way famous saying? Carpe diem, or canape dior. Or something. You know what I mean."

In the end, De agreed to go with me, and even better, to snag a ride from Murray. Only after school the next day, when Murray pulled up, he wasn't alone. The faithful sidekick, Sean, was there, too.

"If this dude is such a major player and all, why are we meeting in some restaurant? Doesn't he have a studio?" Murray was in suspicious mode. And the truth is, I wondered that myself. But I just said, "Maybe he's in between studios."

"Maybe the whole thing is whack" was Sean's contribution to the conversation as he turned up the volume on the Coolio CD. De just rolled her eyes.

Zuma Sushi turned out to be a total trendoid hangout off the Pacific Coast Highway in Malibu. We had no trouble finding it and less trouble finding Buff Bobby. He more than lived up to his nickname. A peek at his way exposed pecs was total confirmation. That Polo Sport tank top was a nice touch. I was getting good vibes about this already.

"Are you Bobby?" I asked, walking up to him. I'd worn an Agnes B. crop-top and Bebe mini-skirt, to dispel any qualms Buff Bobby might have about my fitness qualifications.

"Cher . . . ?" he said haltingly, getting up from his chair, and eyeballing De, Murray, and Sean, who were right behind me.

"In the exercise-friendly flesh," I said to remind him of our first conversation, and extended my hand. Which he automatically shook. I noticed the absence of jewelry. Specifically, no wedding ring. "And these are my friends," I said, turning to indicate De, Murray, and Sean. "They're typical teens like me. Guys, this is Bobby Van Hoosen."

"So, okay, you brought friends," Bobby said. I couldn't tell if he thought this was a good thing, or not.

Once we were all settled with our lemon-laced Arrowheads, Pellegrinos, and Evians, Buff Bobby asked, "Who's hungry?" Without waiting for an answer, he added, "I recommend the special sushi and sashimi deluxe sampler. You get a taste of everything that way."

"Sounds choice, I'll have that, too," I said, flashing a blinding smile at him. I noted that it was the most expensive thing on the menu.

De started to order some chirashi puffer until Murray broke in with the news flash, "That's raw, woman. That makes you hurl."

"Don't tell me what I do or do not like, Murray," De growled. "I'll make my own choices. I can do without your input."

"Just trying to save you from having to send it back, is all. I know you, Miss Dionne. You'll take one look at that raw squiggly thing on your plate and you'll be like, 'Aaah! Get it away!' "

I began to panic: a De and Murray fight right here? In front of Buff Bobby? Like, how totally immature would that look?

My concern was misplaced. What was I thinking? No one did immature better than Sean. While De and Murray were arguing, Sean was doing his best to flirt with the waitress. "What do you recommend, homegirl?" He was eyeballing her instead of the menu. "What here's got the flava? In a cooked-all-the-way-through sense?" Sean was trying to be all casual, tilting back in his seat. Make that, way back. As in, too far back. Just as the waitress was suggesting the California roll, the chair slipped from under him. Sean went flying and crashed to the floor. Which Murray found irresistibly, stomach-grippingly, designer-water-spewing-from-his-nose hysterical.

I looked at Buff Bobby, who looked astounded. I shrugged my shoulders, doing my best to convey "I barely know them."

Just then a beeper went off. We all checked, but it turned out to be Bobby's. He glanced at the number but made no move to return the call. I looked at him quizzically. "Just a client," he said. "I'll call back later."

It was De who got the train back on track.

"So, Bobby, what exact kind of fitness routines do you espouse? I mean, is there a specific regime you adhere to? Are you like, some kind of abs expert or something?"

Bobby looked from De to me. I couldn't be sure, but it occurred to me that he wasn't expecting an interrogation. Still, he didn't blink. "Well, of course, tight abs are part of it. But, uh, my regime, as you say, is more toward overall body sculpting. You need to work all your muscle groups equally. You can't expect to be fit just by zeroing in on one area—"

"You go to school to learn this stuff?" Murray interrupted.

Bobby turned to him. "More like on-the-job training, if you know what I mean."

De jumped in, all suspicious, "So it's not as if you have, say, a degree in exercise physiology or anything like that."

Bobby looked surprised. "It's something I've thought about, maybe somewhere down the line, but things are going so well, I don't know if it makes sense to stop and go back to school. I mean, you know, I have the momentum now."

"The momentum. So who exactly have you trained?" De narrowed her eyes.

Bobby smiled. "Well, not to name drop, but it all started with Michael Ovitz's cousin, who liked me and spread the word. Then I helped Aerosmith's manager build stamina. Halle came in for a toning session, and all these TV stars followed, including ABC's entire TGIF lineup. You might be surprised, but Urkel has real muscle definition underneath those costumes he wears. Anyway, then Jennifer Aniston came down, and she recommended me to her friends . . ."

"So let me get this straight." Murray had jumped to attention here. "You're saying you trained Halle Berry—my girl from *The Flintstones*—and the whole cast of *Friends?*"

"Not the monkey," Bobby said with a wink at me.

"So where's your studio, man?" It was amazing how quickly Sean went from imbecile to impertinent. But Bobby didn't blink.

"Up to this point, I've held sessions at other people's facilities. Eventually, I'd like to open my own, a sort of one-stop body shop, but that's future tense. For now, I'm thinking a video should be my next step. So when Fabianne called about Cher, I thought this just might be the thing. I mean, I have worked behind the scenes on the Crunch series, and The Firm . . ."

As Bobby began to roll his personal credits, I tried to listen, but all I heard was his body language—his tanned, sinewy shoulders and sun-bleached blond hair, which today was falling adorably over his cloudless sky blue eyes. Then, Bobby fixed his cerulean blues on me. I was mesmerized.

"This idea of a fitness video for teenagers is so prime, Cher. The way I see it"—Bobby spread his hands across the table—"it would be similar in concept to the hottest videos that are out now, the ones fronted by supermodels. They themselves aren't the experts, they're guided by a trainer."

"So let me get this straight," De interrupted. "You've been looking for a supermodel to do a video with, but you couldn't find one?"

Bobby eyeballed De. "No, not at all. People are over that whole and-a-supermodel-will-lead-us kind of thing. I'm looking for a fresh approach, something that'll be the next big thing, and one that might actually help people." Bobby paused and then added, almost bashfully, "Of course, it wouldn't hurt, while I'm at it, to make some money, too."

A prospect no one at *this* table voiced opposition to.

Bobby proceeded with his vision for the video. "What I had in mind was something very cutting edge. Something teenagers won't be bored by. I mean, it wasn't all that long ago that I was a teenager."

De jumped in. "Just how old are you, Bobby?"

He looked surprised by her question but didn't dodge it. "I'm twenty-four—so like I said, not that far removed. In fact, I'm working on some routines that combine club dancing with fitness."

As Bobby rattled off the exercises—"I was thinking a little power funk, a little hip-hop funk, a little cardio funk, some low-impact aerobics, and high energy moves"—I calculated, nine years between us. Not an unbridgeable gap.

Suddenly, Murray had his own vision. "You got something planned for the distribution angle?" he asked. It's funny about Murray. The minute he smells money to be made, homeboy disappears and entrepreneur boy emerges.

Where the video would be sold was something Bobby had yet to consider. After all, Bobby's a fitness artist, not a salesman. But Murray is. While Murray got off on a business tangent, I looked out the window. The sun had just started its descent over the ragingly azure ocean of Malibu. The rays were piercing the window and falling right across Bobby's chest. How perfect was this going to be? Me, De, all of us together, on a way important, lifestyle-improving project? And with Buff Bobby in the picture . . . Well, as Fabianne said, "Who knows what might develop?"

Okay, so I hadn't like, taken scrupulous mental notes on all he was saying. But I got the important part about our perfect partnership. Buff Bobby had the know-how to be the master-crafter of the video. My t.b.'s and I would be symbols of America's youth. Together we could rock the industry.

"All I need is your participation, Cher," Bobby was

saying, gazing intently into my eyes. "And, if possible, some help with the start-up capital."

I was so psyched on the ride home that I was actually singing out loud to "Exhale (Shoop, Shoop)." I was halfway through the first verse when I noticed De wasn't singing along with me.

"Zup, De? I thought this was your song."

Murray answered for her. "It isn't the song, Cher. I know my woman like a rap verse. And she is just not down with the whole Buff Bobby video thing."

"When I need you to answer for me, Murray, I'll send a smoke signal," De lashed out.

"Is that true, De? You're not with me on this?" I asked, surprised.

"There's something about that man and this whole project I just do not trust," De said deliberately. "I don't like him."

Suddenly, I was buggin'. "You know, De, if it weren't for snap judgment, you'd have no judgment at all."

"Whatever," De answered, turning away.

# Chapter 5

That night Buff Bobby called. "Just to tell you how pumped I am, Cher."

"Totally. I could see that," I said, visualizing his rampantly pumped upper arms.

Bobby paused for a sec, then went on, "I mean, Fabianne said you were in good shape, but those abs! Those deltoids! That musculature! Man, you are so perfect," he said in a soft voice—especially for someone with such a hard body.

"You don't think it's a problem that I'm not, like experienced in videos?" I asked coyly.

"No experience necessary. I'll be there guiding you every stretch of the way. I don't know about you, but I'm feelin' the burn already. But I want to make sure you see the total picture."

I pictured Bobby's total Baldwin quotient.

He continued. "Fabianne did mention, when she told me about you—maybe she was overstepping her bounds—but anyway, there's an investment angle here. She said that maybe your father might want to invest?"

Before I could really ponder that, Bobby clarified. "Naturally, he'd share in the profits, too. And this could be huge. Profit-city."

"That sounds . . . possible," I said, a little unsure of how to respond.

Bobby plowed on. "Tell you what. I'll have the contracts drawn up, and I'll messenger them over tomorrow afternoon for your father to look at. What's the address?"

Okay, so I wasn't exactly sure how I felt about that whole investment angle. And of course, the mention of contracts had only one high impact on me: the vision of furiously knitted eyebrows and popping neck veins. Daddy.

"Um, sure, send them over," I said, giving Bobby the address, "but it might take a little time to get them signed." What I meant was, to break this news to Daddy and get his approval.

"Well, not too much, I hope," Bobby said softly. "So let's take another meeting, go over some details. This time, just the two of us, okay?"

I agreed to meet Buff Bobby as soon as I'd had a chance to interface with Daddy. That, as it turned out, happened sooner than expected.

"Cher! Get in here! What is this?" I'd just gotten home from school the next day and the way Daddy was yelling? Industrial-strength earplug alert! Daddy was frenetically waving a sheaf of papers.

"Yes, Daddy?" I said innocently, wondering, could Bobby have really gotten the contracts over so quickly? Like, before I'd had a chance to convince Daddy about the worthiness of this project?

I didn't have long to wonder, as Daddy continued with his tirade. "This is a contract with *your* name on it! Spelled wrong. What kind of idiot writes *Share?*"

I was just about to answer that, but the steam coming out of Daddy's ears told me I'd better wait. Besides, Daddy didn't pause for a breath.

"This came by messenger this morning. It's an agreement to participate in some cockamamie exercise video. Which, I might add, needs a sizable investment from me! Is there anything you want to tell me? That is, before I put it through the shredder?" Uh-oh, Daddy was screeching toward postal and I hadn't even gotten a word in yet.

"Don't do that, Daddy! I can explain everything. And when I'm finished—just wait, you'll be so proud of me." I flashed what I hoped was an obedient yet competent smile.

"So you actually know something about this?" Daddy's eyebrows knitted dangerously as he swung around from behind the desk.

"Of course I do, Daddy. Only I didn't know the contracts would be here so soon." One look at Daddy's pulsing vein told me I'd better amend that to, "I mean, so prematurely."

Daddy looked at his watch. "You've got three minutes, Cher. And this better be good."

"How about a snack, Daddy," I started. "I can have Lucy whip up—"

"You don't have time for me to have a snack, Cher. Tick-tock."

So I sat Daddy down and told him everything. About what a monster idea the video was. About my contribution to teenkind. About all my friends teaming up to do this together. I was just getting to the fashion end of it when Daddy interrupted, "And who did you say hooked you up with this illiterate? This Van Hooter character?"

"Van Hoosen. Bobby. Tscha, it's totally on the level, Daddy. He's a professional colleague"—okay, so I was stretching it a teensy bit—"of Fabianne's."

"Really? And just who is Fabianne?" Since Daddy rarely, well, okay, never, had time for a massage, he didn't know Fabianne personally. Just by way of her bills.

"Doy, Daddy, she's on staff. She works for us. In the stress-reduction department, which, now that I think of it, you should really try."

"You're getting off track, Cher. And you have exactly seventy seconds left to explain this."

"Doing the video will be way entrepreneurial, and aren't you always saying what a good head I have for business? This is my first step into the business world."

"Your business is school, Cher. If you want an after-school job, I can arrange one for you." With that, Daddy got up and started back for his desk.

I had no choice but to use my ace in the hole. "Think of it this way, Daddy. If you go along with this, you'll be investing in me. And you know I'll come through for you. There'll be major profits coming in from the video. In fact, for the first time in my life, I'll be making money, not just spending it."

Daddy looked suspicious. "I'll believe that when I see it."

And then I hit him with my best shot. "Besides, if you want the truth, I really got the idea from you. Remember when you told me about that niche thing? Well, I thought about it and decided you were right. My friends are looking for their niches, and so am I. And I found one that fits like an Alaïa. And there's enough room for all my friends, too. It's so totally chronic, Daddy. Don't you agree?"

Just then Daddy's secretary beeped in. "Mr. Shapiro's on the line, and he says it's urgent."

"To that schnorrer, a pastrami on rye is urgent," Daddy barked into the speaker phone. "Tell him to hold!" With that, Daddy turned back to me.

"Look, Cher, I still don't know what all this is about. But I will not commit one penny to anything nor sign anything until I go through it thoroughly."

"Duh, Daddy, I was planning on bringing it to you."

"So we'll have to table this whole thing." With that, he punched the speaker phone, "Shapiro? You there? What the—"

Quietly, I planted a kiss on Daddy's cheek and swirled around. I had him in the palm of my hand. As usual.

At nutrition break the next day, I hunted for De, who needed persuading. But as I scoured the quad, my field of vision was suddenly and completely clouded. It wasn't so much Amber, as her hair. It looked like a helmet on steroids. Of course, it did cover a lot of her face, and you can't overestimate the value of that. Unfortunately, she could still talk.

"I heard about your video thing," she sneered, "and I think it's a harebrained idea."

"Speaking of hair, who's the stylist who ax-murdered yours?" I said, wondering how she could have heard about the video so quickly. Amber pretended she hadn't heard my comeback, but she did solve the more important mystery for me.

"Sean is telling the whole school about it, and I have to tell you, the idea reeks."

Sean! What a surprise—not! If I wasn't so busy thinking about how to convince De, I would have figured that out and been better prepared.

Now Amber was all, "If you need something to occupy you, Cher, come and campaign for me. I'm making some real changes in the world. Starting right here, at school."

Amber couldn't have been more transparent if she were wearing a see-through polyamide dress. She was totally buggin' that I might take the spotlight off her. Hello? When was it ever on her?

"Besides," Amber was blabbing on, "if I don't win, we'll be stuck with Brian Fuller for class president. And he's just running so it'll look good on his transcript. While I, Amber Salk, have the purest motivations at heart. And besides, Cher, my campaign should be meaningful to you. After all, we are in the same crowd.

We have the same friends. We are cut from the same cloth," she finished dramatically.

The same cloth? Gag me with a rag.

Amber was running against the school brainiac. Brian, whose idea of interfacing consisted of boring soundbites on RAMs, megahertz, mother boards, and the vagaries of Pentium chips, had the entire nerdzone on his hard drive. As well as the student councilites. And for some reason, I remember hearing that the jocks had been talked into backing him, too. Amber had to put together a coalition of what was left.

"Well, I'm sure you'll have the support of the fashion-impaired, as well as the brain-challenged," I said absently, brushing by her.

My little sidebar with Amber had taken up what was left of nutrition, and I hadn't run into De. I didn't want to page her. I had the rampant need for an interface.

But I did spend the rest of the day trying to figure out what would bring De into the fold. It was in Miss Geist's class that I got the idea. Not from anything she said, but just by looking around the room. Along the back wall were posters. One had a Hands Across America theme and was riddled with a multicultural spectrum of people. Brainstorm.

I was so psyched, I had to get to De ASAP. I barely heard Geist giving out the assignment. I tossed my mini Prada backpack over my shoulder, and darted out into the hallway to find De.

When I found her, just before last period, she was alone. Her new "sisters" were nowhere in sight. I got straight to the point.

"No one has done this before, De. I mean, do you know one teenager who has her own exercise video? Think about all the hotties who are video stars now. There's Claudia. Kathy. Tawny. Geritol generation to the max. And Jane or Richard? Like, how do *you* spell Jurassic? Do any of them represent us? Do any of them represent *you?*"

I didn't have to connect the dots for De. Although there were exercise videos fronted by such divas as Donna Richardson and Victoria Johnson, there were none by any African-American teenage Betty. If De came in with me, she could be the first. The original. And nothing buttered De's muffin better than being original.

"Our video will be brutally chronic, girlfriend," I went on. "It will so totally represent all of us. In all our individuality. A rainbow coalition of the best teenage America has to offer." I knew I was on the blabberville express, but I didn't want to give De the chance to turn me down.

"And let's not forget the fashion angle of this. We will have killer ensembles. We'll all be working together to promote self-esteem *and* firm abs. A total 'we are the world' event. We can even include some songs from *Exhale* to exercise to." Okay, so the music hadn't come up yet, but I would have said anything to get De into it. Finally, she cut in.

"So what you're saying, Cher, is that we'll all be in this together? Not just you and me and our old crowd, but Shaniqua, Essence, and Shawana, too?"

"Achievable, girlfriend." I flashed her a grin, ignoring the pain of that "our old crowd" remark. "Just come in with me and help me plan it."

"What about that Buff Bobby dude?" De demanded. "He thinks he's all that and a bag of chips. What'll he have to say about my involvement?"

"Tscha! I'll take care of him. He's totally trustworthy and wants us all to be involved, not just me." Okay, so I wasn't so sure about that last part. Yet.

De looked away. But only for a second. Then she gave me one of her old De smiles. The gentle kind she did not normally share with the rest of the world.

"You know, I never told you this Cher, but whenever we'd work out together? I used to picture myself out there, in front of the camera, showing everyone the way." De giggled. "Total Gumbyhead, huh?"

"Not even. Not now." I looked De straight in the eyes. "This is the real deal, girlfriend. We've got the chance to make it happen. But I can't—" I needed De to understand how critical this was. I totally bared my soul.

"I *won't* do it without you, De. You have always been the wind beneath my palm trees. Or something. If you say no, I'll drop the whole idea."

"Well, then"—De's eyes danced when she looked at me—"you leave me no choice."

For a split second I got worried. But then De raised her hand to high five me in that limp-wristed way we always did it in the old days. This time, I exhaled.

Over the next few days, everything came together. Like when your outfit matches your car.

Once I had De's thumbs-up, Murray got revved. It

was like he needed her approval or something. Lately, I noticed Murray walking on eggshells around De. Her *Waiting to Exhale* phase was affecting him, too. De and Murray were hardly even fighting anymore. But once she'd put her stamp of approval on the video project, Murray got back on his distribution track and was all, "I'm gonna be taking meetings with Blockbuster and Tower."

As usual, Tai was a pushover. Even though it took her a while to get it.

"So you're gonna, like, do makeovers on video?" she said. "That's cool."

"Not exactly, Tai," I answered, "but remember when De and I chose some workout videos back when we were helping you . . . assimilate?" If I'd jogged Tai's memory, she showed no sign of it. "Remember the workout tapes we used? *Buns of Steel?* Well, now, we're going to do our own. For teenagers, by teenagers.

"And you want me to be involved?" Tai seemed surprised.

"Well, duh, Tai. Last time I looked, you were a teenager. Not to mention, last time I looked, you were a t.b." At this, Tai looked confused. Then I added, "Look, I know you're all involved in helping canine-kind and all—"

"I'm training Peabo for his life's work, to guide a blind person."

"Well, then, being part of my exercise video expands on that whole guiding thing. You'll be guiding an entire generation. Your own!"

Tai shrugged. "Um, well, okay, I guess. Peabo takes

up most of my spare time. It's a major responsibility. But I'd do anything to help you."

I put my arm around Tai and said softly, "Thanks. I knew I could count on you."

My friends were all in place. All I needed was Daddy. Okay, so I know that patience is like, all virtuous and stuff, but what if Daddy forgot about it? I couldn't take that chance. I decided to just go for it.

"I don't mean to bother you, Daddy," I said one night after a total comfort food fest I'd had Lucy prepare to butter him up. "But did you happen to go over that exercise video contract yet?"

Daddy wiped his face with the linen napkin and turned to me. "It just so happens, I have."

"You have?" I couldn't disguise the surprise and joy in my voice. "Thank you, Daddy! You're the best!"

"Not so fast, Cher." Uh-oh, was it even remotely possible Daddy might put the kibosh on this? He couldn't, not when all my friends were ready to get back together.

"But we are going ahead with this, Daddy? Aren't we?" I gave him a pleading look.

"I will—" he started.

"Yay, Daddy!" I jumped up and hugged him.

"I will invest in this because I believe there may be profit possibilities. As for your participation, I will allow you to do this, *but*"—Daddy started to raise his voice, so I sat back down—"there are a few caveats here."

"Name them, Daddy, and I am so totally there."

First, I was not allowed to let my grades slip. "Not one iota," Daddy warned. "I'll be looking for proof."

"Solid," I agreed.

Next, all my chores had to be done. This needed clarification since I didn't exactly have any chores. But Daddy was prepared for that. He gave me one.

"I want you to help with the Zinger depo. I've got all these law students working on it, but none of them has your eye for detail. So I want you to go through some files and look for inconsistencies in the records. I'm going to give you the files later. Just remember, you cannot lose or misplace anything. The files are crucial to the case."

"Totally done, Daddy. You can so count on my eye for detail. In fact, I'll use both of them." I winked at Daddy.

"Do you understand where I'm going with this, Cher?" Daddy didn't give me a chance to respond. "I will not allow this video thing to take up all your time."

"Don't worry, Daddy. The only thing I'll have less time for is shopping."

As if he hadn't heard me, he continued, "I'll want to meet this Van Hoser character, too. I did an entire background check on him, but I still want you to bring him here before you get started."

Daddy did a background check on Bobby? It shouldn't have surprised me. But Bobby must have passed if Daddy was agreeing to this.

"You'll meet him ASAP, Daddy." I was about to thank him prodigiously when he said, "And one more caveat. I've asked your brother to oversee this."

My brother? I didn't even have a— No! He couldn't mean . . .

"I can't be everywhere, Cher, and the first rule of

business is: never trust anyone. Just because this Van Hopper hasn't had any felony arrests doesn't mean we can trust him. Besides, Josh has already gone over the contract. Drew up some excellent codicils. For your protection. I agreed with all of them."

"Josh! As if I need a baby-sitter!" I totally harrumphed. Maybe the person Daddy doesn't trust is me.

"That's it, Cher." Daddy had that finality tone in his voice. "Those are the conditions and they are non-negotiable. You agree, I invest, I sign."

I was less than ecstatic. The Josh thing was like a tiny but perceptible stain on my new Calvin. But I knew to keep my eye on the prize. The main thing was, Daddy had said yes. And if I couldn't minimize the presence of the pain-in-the-gut stepsib, I was not worthy of the name Cher Horowitz.

# Chapter 6

Even though Daddy had insisted on meeting Bobby, and I was supposed to keep Josh in the loop, I figured there was plenty of time for all that. Besides, Daddy could be kind of intimidating if you weren't adequately prepared. So for our meeting, I arranged for Bobby to pick me up at school. He pulled up in his lipstick red retro two-seater Dodge Stealth. Chronic, in a low-to-the-ground kind of way.

"Hungry, Cher?" Bobby asked as I crouched to let myself into the car. It seemed the only way to do it was butt first. Bobby was wearing Adidas shorts and Ray-Ban ellipse orbs. I guessed he'd just come from training some way famous star. "How 'bout we hit the Trat for a snack? That cool with you?"

"Whatever," I said.

The Trat turned out to be Trattoria Amici, a way

mauve new hot spot right in my nabe, Beverly Hills. Once we were settled in our booth, I began to describe to Bobby how Daddy had agreed and the contracts were signed, and most significantly, how all my friends were with me on this. Bobby was way pumped about the contract thing. When our lemon-laced Pellegrinos arrived, Bobby raised his glass. "A toast," he said, "to us and our project. I really think that we can do something special, start a whole new trend. Who knows? Maybe an entire line of videos!"

"Totally," I agreed, clinking my glass with his.

Bobby began to describe how the video would be done. "It looks easier than it really is, Cher," he warned. "It's not just a class. There's more involved than just learning the exercises. Like a million details."

"I am so up for this. My t.b.'s and I totally want to be involved in all aspects," I said enthusiastically.

The corners of Bobby's shapely mouth turned down for a split sec, but then he said, "Naturally, I'll handle most of it, but don't sweat it, you'll be more than just a figurehead. Of course, you do have a great figure," he added.

When the waiter came, Bobby ordered straw and hay pasta while I decided to stick with a salad of field greens. No sense jeopardizing my great figure.

Then Bobby whipped a piece of paper out of his shorts pocket. It was way crumpled. He gave me a kind of embarrassed grin and pushed a lock of shiny hair off his forehead. "Okay, so I made a list of some points to go over with you."

My heart quickened. I don't know why, but for some

reason Bobby's drawing up a list for me seemed incredibly sweet. Also, the way he kept ignoring his beeper. Who was beeping him so much? Probably some of his star clients. And Bobby's, like, ignoring Urkel for me.

"Uh-hmm," he cleared his throat and read. "First, there's the exercise routines. I'll have to teach them to you. So that means rehearsals. Lots of them."

That sounded way righteous to me.

"I'm renting times at a studio in the Valley."

The Valley? Okay, whatever.

"My people are accessing studios, camera crews, and a director," Bobby read.

"People?" I said, a little confused, "You have people?"

Bobby looked up from his note. "Well, sure, Cher. It costs a mountain of moolah to put together a project like this. That's why I have backers and investors." He fixed his cerulean blues on me intently. "They've come up with a budget that we'll work within."

Budget? A word not normally found in my personal vocabulary. But the way Bobby was looking at me? Hello? All I could do was smile. And keep smiling. His shoulders were brutally broad, and what I could see of his chest? Excessively smooth. I pictured my head resting on it. I was so busy picturing, I barely heard Bobby continuing, "Then there's the location. I'd rather not do it in a studio if we can help it. We'll need a writer, too, plus we'll have to get the rights to whatever music I choose." He grinned at me. "All that stuff is money-intense."

The mention of money snapped me back into reality. Then I had a brainstorm. "Bobby?" I said thoughtfully. "What if I could get us the rights to use whatever music we want for free?"

Bobby narrowed his long-lashed peepers, and I noticed a scrunchy little crease in his forehead. "How?"

"Just let me work on it, okay?" I said coyly. Until it was a fait accompli, I didn't want to say exactly. But I did have something else to add. "I know you're the exercise expert and all, but there is one viciously important element I could bring to the relationship."

"You're bringing yourself, Cher. What else do we need?" Bobby's smile was dazzling. It was hard to stay on track, but I did.

"No, what I mean is, the whole fashion angle. You haven't mentioned that."

Bobby looked perplexed. "Fashion? Angle? I'm not following you."

"Duh, what we'll be wearing in the video. It has to be rampantly right or the whole thing will be bogus." I was also thinking that the money saved on the music could totally go toward the ensembles.

Bobby took his time answering me. "Okay, well, right. If you want to, uh, think about it, that's cool. Whatever blows your hair back." With that, he shrugged his sinewy shoulders, lifted a forkful of pasta to his lips, and hungrily wolfed it down.

As we talked and ate, I tried to think of a way to prepare Bobby for meeting Daddy. "So when's our next meeting?" I asked.

"No more meetings, cutie. The next time we meet

will be at our first rehearsal. Soon as I get studio time locked in, I'll call you."

Bobby called me cutie. I forgot all about Daddy.

The thought of needing something from Jesse Fiegenhut was severely unthrilling. He's the Crew and all, but Jesse's ego is so hyperinflated, they had to build an extra closet in his bedroom for it. Doing anything that could puff up his opinion of himself might actually make him explode. But I can do more than spell *pragmatic.* I even know what it means.

I came upon my quarry in the Quad the next day. He was all linen Pronto-Uomo, perched on the edge of a bench. The cellular was scrunched between his shoulder and jaw, leaving his hands free to rifle through a stack of CDs. I came up behind him and gently removed the cell from its way uncomfortable position. With one hand, I held it up to Jesse's ear, allowing him to continue his conversation more comfortably. With the other hand, I massaged his shoulder. Jesse barely turned around. He acted as if random Bettys cater to his every need all the time. Which, mainly, they do.

When he turned to me, he squinted and said, "Cher! Didn't realize it was you. Uh, thanks. Do me a favor, press Power and turn it off." He was about to return to his CDs, when I came around and sat down next to him. I was wearing a micro-mini A/X and ribbed V-neck BCBG Max Azria.

"Your newest freebies?" I said, indicating the stack with the Promotional Use Only stickers on them. He nodded. "Can I see?" I asked.

"You care about my CDs?" Jesse's arched eyebrows shot up. This was not an area I'd ever expressed interest in before. He tried to guess my agenda. "Need a gift to impress a new boyfriend?"

"Tscha! Jesse, give me a little credit. I'm—" I was about to say "sincerely interested," but I hung an abrupt U-ie and decided on the truth. Sort of.

"Okay, I give. You know me too well. But no, it's not a boy—doy! And it's not the actual CDs I care about. It's more that I need to access a musical guru. Someone rampantly familiar with all aspects of today's most chronic beats."

"And you thought of me, naturally. Why?" he asked suspiciously.

So Jesse hasn't heard about the video. Or if he has, he hasn't put two and two together. I explained about the video, being careful to include only the most pressing need-to-know parts. I needed to make Jesse feel important, and let him think I was doing him the props, by including him in the most white-hot new happening thing.

"So I was thinking of going straight to Sony for the music, when I saw you sitting here," I was saying. "And then I thought, hang on, Sloopy! This is supposed to be an 'our generation' thing. What if I give a member of our generation a chance to participate. In an integral, wholly consequential way. Who better than you?"

Jesse's look was blanker than usual. So I drew him a picture. "What if you help choose the music we'll exercise to, and then"—I was about to complete the transaction—"see if your father can secure the rights."

And the Oscar for most convincing rendition of "I just thought of of this now" goes to . . . me! Jesse was Play-Doh in my hands. He got so excited, he actually jumped up, sending the CDs crashing to the ground.

"Monster idea, Cher! We can go with Garbage. No, maybe Rancid. But Butthole Surfers are coming out with some raging stuff."

Then he stopped and sat down next to me in a total I'm-in-your-space sense. "Let's have it, Cher. Why did you really come to me?"

Uh-oh, was I about to be exposed for the total freebie-seeker I was? It turned out, no. Jesse wasn't *that* intuitive. He put his arm around me and pulled me close. I resisted but not that much.

"If I supply the music, this means we'll be working together? Spending a lot of time in close quarters, won't we? You know, most girls just flirt and stuff. They're so obvious. But you're different, Cher. You've always had style."

I didn't answer. Jesse thought I'd enlisted him because I was actually sprung on him? As if! I was about to disabuse him of that notion, when I realized that maybe now wasn't the best time. I mean, the health and welfare of an entire generation was at stake—not to mention more money for brutally hot ensembles.

If Jesse had been clueless about the video, he was the only one. Is there like anything more powerful and speedy than the grapevine? Like, memo to the information highway. I could barely step out of class before being accosted by my peers. Each and every designer-clad one wanted to be involved. I wasn't sure how, but maybe I *could* make some room in that chorus line section of the video for them.

At lunch I checked into my usual reserved spot. All my homies surrounded me and then some. Jackson Doyle awoke briefly from his coma to intone, "Yo, your Cher-ness. That video-rama thing is singularly excellent. You'll be today's total video-vixen and we'll be more famous than those dudes on *The Real World.*"

Tai agreed with him. "Yeah, Jackson is right. The *Real World* cast is like only around for one season, but we'll be on video for perpituitary. That's so cool." She looked at Jackson. Their eyes actually locked.

They weren't the only ones at the table talking video. It was like, *the* topic. My homies were all, at this moment, pitching ideas like hissy fits. "No, no, the butt thrusts should go first," Shaniqua was insisting.

"Anyone knows the ab crunches come before that," Essence contradicted.

She and Shawana got up to demonstrate. "Get your rear in gear, girlfriend," Shaniqua yelled. "Shape that booty, girl!"

I watched them and wondered, Could this day get any more golden? When Amber ambled over, I got my answer. Not even. Her fashion indiscretion today? Let me count the violations. Accessory overload coupled with VPL: visible panty line.

I rolled my eyes at De. "How does she do that?" I asked.

"It's a gift," De answered.

"Hi, guys," Amber drawled. "Shove over?" Without waiting for anyone to do so, she slipped in between Tai and Summer and set down her tray on our large round table. "I want to try out my speech on you." When no one responded, she added, "May I remind you, I am running for class president. And you are my constituents."

"The only thing you should be running for is cover," I said automatically.

"Actually, Cher, it's really you I want to talk to," she said, ignoring my dis. "It's about your video."

I would have let her know that her input was like, not on my required reading list, but Amber actually said something merit-worthy.

"I've come up with a fabuloso idea. Why not film it right here, in our very own open-area quad? You won't find a more typical teenage locale and that way, *tout d'America* can appreciate us, class leaders and all." She winked—at I don't know who—and added, "And with my clout, I could get the administration's approval. It's only a matter of time until I'm elected, after all."

This was way tragic. A killer idea—and Ambu-lame came up with it? The Quad! Bobby had said he didn't want to shoot in a studio. The Quad was roomy and aesthetically pleasing, especially in the soft glow of a smoggy California day. Oh, and one more thing. We might not have to pay for its use.

Ker-chink! Ker-chink! Ker-chink redux. The clothes budget just inflated.

I was already logging massively long days, and we hadn't even started the video. It took, like, halfway through *Melrose Place* to get through all the messages on my voice mail. Not to mention, rifling through the stack of faxes. I wasn't even going near my E-mail. Everyone in my immediate universe had an idea for the video.

I was still listening to like, the forty-fifth message, when I felt weird vibes. I was not alone! I whirled around to face the intruder in the doorway of my bedroom. Josh!

"What are you doing here?" I demanded, surveying my own personal Birkenstock buddy.

"Well, excuse me for crashing your Touch-Tone moment," he said, "but if I remember correctly, you and I were getting together tonight to work on your father's deposition. I was supposed to give you instructions, and you were supposed to be clueing me in about the video."

I was blank. I totally did not remember that . . . oops, my bad. As I was rushing out to school this morning, Daddy did say something about Josh. But at the mention of his name, I must've zoned out.

"You didn't forget, did you? I know your bubble brain is awfully crowded these days," he said snidely.

"Not even, " I lied. "I was just wrapping up here, and then I was coming down to work with you."

"Really?" he looked skeptical. "Well, I'll be in your father's office waiting."

I ran a quick brush through my hair and threw on sweats. Ordinarily, I only strut around in cute little outfits. But that's when there's someone to appreciate them. Josh is so totally no one. When I got downstairs, he was on the couch in Daddy's office, highlighter in hand, intently eyeballing a stack of papers spread out on the mahogany coffee table. Flannel-less, Josh's biceps were exposed. When did they get so developed? In philosophy class? I don't think so.

"How gracious of you to clear time in your busy schedule for this," Josh said sarcastically, looking up and motioning that I should sit down next to him. He glanced at my sweats, arched his eyebrows, but didn't say anything.

Then he cleared his throat. "Okay, here are the fax, E-mail, and cellular records of the communication between Zinger and his partners for 1995." Josh was all business. "It's Mel's theory that those communications were held after hours and on Sundays, which would prove—"

I yawned. Okay, so I knew it was, like, a way inappropriate moment. But I couldn't help it.

"Am I keeping you awake, Cher? Because if you're too tired for this, I can tell Mel—"

I snapped to attention. "Excuse me? You can tell Mel what? That you didn't have the patience to spend ten minutes with me explaining this stuff? Just go on, Josh. I'm on this."

"Not as much as you're on that inane little video thing, I bet," he said.

"Inane! As if! I'm doing something to improve all of teenkind," I said with major conviction. "The lives of today's teens will be better because of me."

But Josh was all, "What are you calling it, Midriff Madness? Thigh Anxiety?"

"I wouldn't expect you to understand, Josh."

Josh gave me a way steady gaze, and then got back to the depo directions. "When you're done highlighting, divide them into piles of strictly fax communications, then E-mail print-outs, and then cellular records. Don't mix up the piles, or we'll have to redo everything."

"Okay, is that all?" This time I stifled a yawn but got up to leave.

"No, it isn't, Cher. Sit down and spare me a few of your precious minutes. Tell me what's really happening with the video. I promised your father I'd oversee this."

Josh acted like he was being forced into this babysitting deal too, so I sat down and gave him the edited version of the 411.

"Well, we're still in development. We do have a monster concept, though."

"Conceptualize for me, Cher."

"Well, it's for teens, by teens. It's the first workout tape that speaks to us, to our generation."

"What does it say? 'Take us to your mall'?" Josh laughed.

"As if! Of course, the fashions will be totally the bomb. But this is something massively different from anything that's ever been done before."

"How do you know?" Josh was suddenly all skeptical and serious.

"How do I know what?"

"That there are no other teen exercise videos out there? Have you done a survey?"

"Hello? Like I need a survey? Don't ask me how I know, I just know."

"If you haven't even seen what's out there, how can you know what has or hasn't been done?" Josh looked at me as if I were an idiot. "It's kind of basic, Cher."

"Well, guess what, Josh? I'm basically going upstairs now. I've got a lot left to deal with tonight."

He shrugged his shoulders but didn't say anything. When I got to the bottom of the stairs he called out, "Aren't you forgetting something?" I stopped.

"The files, Cher. You left them here."

"I totally knew that," I lied. "I was just coming back for them."

It was way late when I finished my homework and I was majorly trashed. When I'm this zonked, I usually float into the sleep zone immediately, but tonight, something wasn't right. Like when you absent-mindedly mismatch the buttons on your Calvin pajama tops and there's that one buttonless hole. I flipped through my mental remote. I paused on . . . what? Josh? Bingo. *That's* what was bothering me. Not Josh himself, but what he'd said.

It was true. I really wasn't all that familiar with other workout tapes. I mean, beyond knowing their titles. And it did seem like common sense to scan them. Buff Bobby would capably handle the exercises, but if I was truly more than just an empty-brained figurehead, shouldn't I be at least aware?

And then I got another brainstorm. This is a mission

for Team Video. Me and De could totally do a video voyage and surround ourselves in tapes. We could go over them together. And not just from the exercise standpoint. The fashion angle would be right there, too. Righteous.

# Chapter 7

As soon as I got up, I called De. She let me get through my entire spiel before delivering her excuse du jour.

"Sorry, Cher, no can do," she said with less lamentation in her voice than I thought appropriate. "I've got a Women of Empowerment club meeting later."

Had De told me about that club? I didn't remember.

"We're meeting to discuss this book, *Value in the Valley.*"

"Excuse me? De, you can't be serious. There *is* nothing of value in the Valley. It's, like, oxymoronic. Or something."

"You're not listening, Cher," De said with more than a flash of impatience. "The whole title is *Value in the Valley—A Black Woman's Guide Through Life's Dilemmas.*"

"Oh. Well, I agree that any dilemma is magnified when it happens in the Valley, De, but aren't there Cliffs Notes or something you could scan? Then you could come with me and also be prepared for your dilemmas."

A way reasonable compromise. Only De didn't ditto. She refused to interrupt her trek through the valley for one through Blockbuster with me.

I sighed and flopped down on the four-poster, trying to dredge up the energy to go by myself when the phone rang. It had to be De, changing her mind. I'd know her ring anywhere.

"So we'll meet at Blockbuster in thirty, okay?" I said, before she could apologize.

"I'd love to join you, but could you give me an hour?" The voice had a familiar whiny tone. It so did not belong to De. "After all, I need time to prepare," it continued. Amber?

"But tell me first why we're going, Cher. Are you preparing for another lonely Saturday night at home? If you are, I have a better suggestion."

"No, Amber, allow me. I have the best suggestion of all. Clearly, I wasn't expecting you to be calling, so I suggest we hang up and pretend this conversation never happened."

"Excuse me, your Cher-ness. It's clear that whoever you were expecting isn't calling," she said snippily. "So why don't you just tell me why you and I are going to Blockbuster." Amber couldn't disguise the anticipation in her voice.

I flipped over on the bed and drew my knees up to

my chest. The idea of comparing and contrasting exercise videos with Amber was so not what I had in mind. But maybe—am I really considering this?—Ambu-lard might come up with another idea vaguely worth considering.

"Forty-five minutes, Amber. And the one on Wilshire. Be there or be square." I hung up.

My Jeep was out being detailed, so I finagled a ride to Blockbuster from Fred-Ed, the brown-nose law student who'd shown up on a Saturday to work with Daddy. I purposely got to the store early, hoping to do a few laps through the aisles before Amber arrived. No such luck.

Amber was there already, and she was all Versus. A name she unfortunately took literally. Plaid trou, horizontal-striped tank top with a keyhole neckline. I'd long ago decided Amber was a fashion victim too far gone to rescue, but seeing her today was enough to make me reconsider. Maybe I *could* work with her to reclaim her fashionable child inside. If there was one.

Amazingly, Fred-Ed seemed intrigued by Amber. As she advanced toward the Ferrari, he pushed the button that opened my window, leaned over, and said, "This must be the friend you're meeting. Are you going to introduce me?"

I looked at him. Pin-striped, straight-laced, boring law clerk. Then I looked at Amber. Not even. Does not compute. Besides, I wasn't really sure which one this was, Fred or Ed. I paused long enough for them to introduce themselves.

Amber leaned down toward the car window and extended her hand. "Oh, hi, I'm Cher's good friend, Amber Salk," she drawled in her patented faux sincere manner. "Student council president-elect," she lied, as if this tidbit of high school info might impress Fred-Ed.

"A pleasure to meet you, Amber Salk. I'm Fred Eichler. I'm working with Cher's father, Mel."

Their handshake crossed in front of my face. Which made it hard, but not impossible, for me to duck under, open the car door, and dart out. It also forced Amber to back up. But not before drawling an appallingly obvious "Will *you* be picking us up, Freddy?"

"Tell me when," he answered with a broad smile. "I'm sure Mel won't mind me dashing out again."

Amber looked to me for an answer. Turning quickly on my heel, I yelled back, "We'll call. Thanks." With that, I was in the store.

The Fitness section was riddled with a confusing array of titles. I was glad Amber was there. At least she could help tote them to the register. But Amber's mind was elsewhere.

"So, girlfriend, what's the 411 on Fred?" she squealed.

"Get over it, Amber. He's just some boring law drone who brown-noses my father and happens to come equipped with a set of chronic wheels. Which, I might add, is his only attraction."

"I'm not surprised *you* can't see past material things," Amber carped. "*I* think he's a total Baldwin." Before this conversation could meander any further down the road untaken, I started pulling videos off the shelf and said, "Whatever. Time on task, Amber. We're here for a purpose. Let's do it."

The usual designer-equivalent workout tapes were well represented. The entire Claudia Schiffer anthology was here and every Jane Fonda since the Flintstoneage. And judging by the plethora of Richard Simmons tapes, he must have sweated to every oldie ever recorded. There were tapes by others I'd vaguely heard of, Kathy Smith, Denise Austin, and celebrities wandering out of their fields like Paula Abdul, Ali MacGraw, and that Olympic dudess, Flo-Jo.

But there were also tons of shape-ups by random generics. Even the MTV dude Eric Nies was in on the workout action, hip-hop style. "Hmm, one for Murray," I thought, tossing it into the pile Amber and I had started.

Fashion was way underrepresented. The only pale imitations of anything resembling style looked like extended commercials for Nike, Reebok, and ESPN. I wondered if that last one was like DKNY?

We got home carrying four shopping bags each. Unfortunately, we had to pass Daddy's office to get to the Great Room. Amber did not miss the opportunity to flounce in, uninvited. "Hi," she said, looking straight at Fred.

"Who are you?" Daddy thundered, annoyed at the interruption.

Amber froze in fear, so I quickly did the intros and yanked her out of the office and into the Great Room.

We dumped the videos out on the carpet. I immediately felt a burning need for nutrition, so I called for a pizza. But if Amber saw the irony in a cal-fest while viewing exercise videos, she didn't protest.

We began with the mother of all exercise gurus, Queen Jane Fonda and her Step Aerobics.

The first ten minutes were all Jane, talking that in faux breathy way of hers. But then Jane like, tossed the whole thing over to her "great instructors" and disappeared! I guess she burns more fat by counting her money.

Okay, so, like, the exercises themselves. Demonstrated by random dancers, they were way boring. No extra credit for fashion either—a great big honking zero.

The music was tow-up. Talk about uncoordinated! It started off all dino-era disco and then did this total turnaround to . . . wee-haa! Country? Who exactly did Jane think was the market for this? Donna Summer wannabes, trapped in Wynonna's body?

We blew off Jane and went to Richard Simmons—Sweatin' to the Oldies. Richard was leading a bunch of mismatched, gluteally challenged people. They were warming up to "Big Girls Don't Cry." Well, at least the music was appropriate.

As Amber and I tried to follow along, I gained new respect for Richard, who clapped continually and gamely encouraged, "Honey, we're workin' it!" He really is serving people-kind in a wholly nonjudgmental and consequential manner. We had to give Richard major snaps for his undertaking, even if, in the end, we found the exercises a little too frenzied.

Luckily, the pizza came just in time. We needed a break.

"Who's next, Cher?" Amber asked, pizza sauce dripping down her chin.

"Let's try something a little closer to our millennium," I suggested, handing her a napkin. I pulled a tape from the Claudia collection. *"Perfectly Fit Buns."*

Right off, it told you that Claud herself had nothing to do with the routines—they were all choreographed and designed by some random trainer to the stars. But unlike Jane, who couldn't be bothered, this was all Claudia and only Claudia. A treat for her drooling boy fans.

Amber and I mimicked as Claudia demonstrated butt bends, thrusts, and other stuff. But it was hard not to be distracted by Claudia's narration. I appreciate her exotic accent and all, but her rendition of "buttocks" came out more like "bootooks."

On the up side, you had to give Claudia snaps for the location—the beach in St. Bart. Way dramatic, with the waves lapping in the background. She lost points on the fashion front, though. It was Claudia in black leggings and long-sleeved crop top, or Claudia in white leggings and white halter top. Maybe her exercise guru had given her a budget, too?

The music veered dangerously from new agey to substandard TLC. Yanni to yawn-y. Amber and I agreed the whole thing was best appreciated on fast forward.

We advanced to Kathy. By the time we hit Denise, Tamilee, David, and Jake, we were way exhausted. Although we'd certainly got that "one, two, three, four" thing down.

Finally, we popped in Eric Nies's Fitness with Flava videos. "This one has to be more relatable," I said hopefully. "After all, it's sponsored by MTV. Maybe Beavis and Butt-head have a cameo."

Eric, a perfectly fit Baldwin under normal circumstances, was leading a posse of fly girls and dudes in these totally frenetic routines.

"As if anyone's hair would not be trashed after five minutes!" Amber harrumphed, smoothing her own mane.

The music, which included such exercise standards as "Insane in the Brain," added to the general confusion. But it was the fashions that disappointed most. Everyone wore the same thing! Drab black leggings, scoop-neck tanks with giant Adidas logos.

I did learn some very valuable info. Bobby had it right. Most of these videos were masterminded and choreographed by experts, trainers who were like the actual exercise designers. But they all seemed to need some supermodel star power to attract an audience. So that's where I came in. The teen queen of Beverly Hills and her hottie homies. This could work, big time. Daddy could make—what did Bobby call it? "Mountains of moolah." And the biggest bonus? It couldn't miss as a bring-us-back-together project. Well, as soon as I got De and Tai a little more involved anyway.

Bobby called on Sunday. The way he sounded when he said, "You awake, Cher?" made my stomach—I mean, abs—do these total flip-flop thingies.

"Of course I'm up." I was about to tell him how his timing was way ripe, since I was writing down ideas for our video, but he interrupted. "We'll talk later, Cher. I'm in the car and we might get cut off. I just scheduled our first rehearsal. Tuesday night at the Burbank Fitness Forum. Can you be there at seven?"

"Uhm, Bobby? Wait—" I couldn't put off his meeting Daddy any longer. "Could you, uh, come here and pick me up? I mean, it's kind of this thing my dad has about, uh, you know, meeting people?"

Bobby agreed. "Sure. Be ready at six-thirty—and be ready to work it!"

I was just about to tell him that I'd round up De, Tai, and the gang, too, but Bobby had already hung up. And as it turned out, this was getting way predictable. No one could make it anyway.

"Sorry, girlfriend" was De's mantra. "But it's such short notice and I got on to the research committee of our group. We've got a meeting on Tuesday." Tai was similarly occupied. In spite of the prodigious amount of time she'd put in, Peabo wasn't nearly on schedule in his training. "And I have to give him up in three months," she whined. "He still doesn't know 'Come.' Or 'Heel.' And I can't keep him out of the garbage."

At the Quad the next morning I bumped into Murray. "Zup, Murray?" I greeted.

He went directly into business mode. "How's the video comin', Cher? Are we down with it? I need some essentials from you before scheduling my meetings."

Murray was so cute when he was serious. And he was totally serious about his contribution. He'd enlisted his father for help. Together they were making distribution inroads. "But we can't take it to the next level until we get more details," Murray explained. "We need to meet with your Buff Bobby dude."

"Viable," I agreed, "and Bobby's people. He's got people, you know. By the way, Murray, where's your woman?"

"In some meetin' or other, I can't keep it straight." Murray was buggin'. He was seeing less of De than even I was. He led me over to a bench.

"Is something really bad going on, Murray?" Suddenly, I was filled with dread as I felt the cold chill of the concrete bench connect with my bare skin.

"De dumped me, Cher." Murray's voice was shaky with emotion.

"Tscha, Murray. That can't be. De's just—I don't know—journeying. Or something. She'll journey back to you." It was as if he hadn't even heard me.

"At first, she was just ducking me," Murray continued. "She didn't return any of my messages. So last night, I beeped her from her mother's house, so she wouldn't know it was me. She'd have to call back. But when I got on the line, she was like, 'Don't ever beep me again. It's over.'"

"Not even, Murray." I tried to be reassuring. "De and you fight all the time."

"But that's just it, Cher. We weren't fightin'. That's how I knew."

Uh-oh. This was critical. "Well, did she even tell you why?"

"Oh yeah, she did. Somethin' about how she was goin' in all this new direction. About how bein' with me was like defining her or something. And how it's time for her to define herself. She said I wouldn't understand and all."

Which sounded perilously close to what De had said to me.

Murray shook his head. "I don't know. It's true, me and De have been hangin' a long time. Maybe she's right. Maybe it's time to break up."

"Not even!" I replied hotly. This was so rampantly wrong. "Look, Murray. I don't care what journey De is on, and I don't even care about her new friends—I mean, the fashion lapses are something else—but this is big. You and De are so totally meant for each other. I can't allow this to happen."

"You can't *allow* it?" Murray looked at me incredulously. Then he, like, started to trip on me. "First of all, Cher, aren't you the one who's always sayin'"—and here Murray did this totally ridiculous imitation of me—" 'Oh, De, girlfriend, you can do so much better than Murray.' "

"I never said that!" I started. "At least not in that voice. And besides, I never really meant it."

But Murray was off and venting.

"And who do you think you are?" he demanded. "You think *you* can do something about this? I ain't seen you spendin' a whole lot of time with Miss Dionne, either."

Murray had hit close to the bone, but I wasn't about to be distracted. De might have temporarily deserted our friendship, but no way would I let her ditch her true soulmate. So what if I do rag on their relationship from time to time—okay, a lot. But in my heart? Everyone knows they belong together. My mission was rampantly clear here.

Suddenly, I popped up from the bench. "Don't stress, Murray. Leave it to Aunt Cher. I'm working on bringing me and De back together. I'll just add bringing the two of you back to the list. Not a problem."

Murray looked at me suspiciously. But there was something else in his eyes that hadn't been there before. Hope.

Just then Jesse strutted over. "Greetings, my little workout wench," he said, flinging an arm around my shoulder.

"I heard you're doin' the music for the video," Murray said to Jesse. "That true?"

"You heard right, man. Jesse Fiegenhut, musical director, at your service. As we speak, I am lining up the most raging tracks for our little project here."

"You got any African congas happenin'? Or Caribbean calypso?" Sean was suddenly in the frame.

Jesse considered. "That can be arranged. I'll add your request to the list." He whipped out a leather Gucci organizer.

"How about Immature?" Murray suggested.

"Not you, Sean," I jumped in. "The group, not the behavior."

Jesse went on to describe everything he'd lined up so far. "We got Bush. We got Oasis. We're getting the Presidents of the United States of America, Chili Peppers, Mary J. Blige, 2Pac, and maybe Coolio. Then there's Urban Decay—"

Murray stopped him. "I'm cool with the first few, but I ain't down with that last one. Describe."

"Dude? They are the slammin-est." Jesse was way

excited. "They're not even signed yet. Five majors are fightin' over them. They're gonna be the next big thing. And we will have them first."

"What's the music like?" I asked.

"Extremely tomorrow. An angular, angry mash of hard-core metal and funk over cathartic cries."

"Are you sure this sounds, you know, right?" I stopped him. "It's for an exercise video, Jesse, not a soundtrack to a mass homicide."

"Be cool, my sweet Cher-ette. Do I not know what's hot, what's cool, what's jammin', what's slammin'? You picked me to be your man and so I am. The music track alone on this video is gonna bust it. Just wait and see."

Okay, so like Jesse is totally impressed with himself, and under ordinary circumstances I would never encourage him. But after listening to everything he and his father had lined up so far, even I was impressed. Enough to throw my arms around him and give him a major hug. He hugged back.

Before the bell rang for next period, I'd agreed to set up Murray and his dad and Jesse and *his* dad with Bobby and his people. I entered algebra class wearing a major grin. This was so dope. My friends—well, okay, not exactly De and Tai, yet—were so into this. And their contributions were rampantly vital. This was totally the thing to bring us all back together.

Just as I settled into my seat, I caught a major whiff of Ambulosis. "Shopping in Designer Imposters again?" I said, sniffing her perfume.

But Amber waved my comment away. "I've done it, Cher," she said confidently.

"Done what?" I asked, flipping open my notebook.

"As location director for the video—" she started.

"*Excuse me?* As what?"

"Well, since I, Amber Salk, have single-handedly procured the use of our very own Quad for the video location, I think it's only fair that I be credited as location director."

I was startled. Mainly at her hubris, but also, I admit, at her ability to snare the Quad. This was big. And this was free. I was suspicious.

"How'd you do it?" I asked.

"Wouldn't you like to know?" she smiled craftily.

"This has something to do with your campaign, doesn't it, Ambu-lunatic? What'd you do, promise Administration we'd like, clean up or something?"

"Think whatever you want, Cher. Nothing changes the fact that we can use the Quad, and it's all because of me. But, please, don't thank me. After all, as friends, we all support each other in our quests."

We're friends? Stab me repeatedly.

# Chapter 8

On Tuesday, I wanted to impress Bobby with how ready I could be, so when the chimes rang at six-thirty in real time, I had all my makeup on. I was still deciding between the one-piece Aero Dynamics with the criss-cross back straps and the bike shorts/halter top combo, so I yelled downstairs, "Lucy? Can you get it? I'll be right there!"

When I made my entrance a few minutes later, I saw Bobby, hands stuffed in his pockets, standing hesitantly at the door. Like he was afraid to come in any farther. Okay, so there was good reason for that.

Daddy was bellowing from his office, "Cher! Who's at the door? That exercise shyster? Bring him in here!"

I gave Bobby a reassuring smile, took his hand, and led him to the slaughter—I mean, to Daddy. This was totally not going to be great. And the unexpected presence of the ex-stepbrother exacerbated it.

Daddy eagle-eyed Bobby. "Where are you taking my daughter?" he demanded. Formal introductions and small talk were not Daddy's strong suit—not when a guy was coming to pick me up.

Bobby stammered. "To—to—the studio. Uh, didn't Cher tell you?"

"*You* tell me," Daddy growled.

My save. "We're going to Bobby's studio in Burbank for the rehearsal. You remember, Daddy, right?" I purred. Daddy ignored me and glared at Bobby.

"And who else is going to be in this studio? It better be filled with people, because there's no way I let my daughter out the door with you otherwise."

To me, again. "Duh, Daddy. Of course it will be! It's an exercise studio. You know, lots of people working out, doing bench presses, lifting weights. And stuff." As I pantomimed the last part, I calculated a fifty percent chance of this being true. And I so desperately hoped Bobby wouldn't be brain-impaired enough to contradict me. I'll never know, because Daddy didn't give him a chance. He looked at my shorts and halter ensemble instead and barked, "Get dressed. You're not going out like that."

"I was just going up to put sweats on," I said quickly. Not part of the original equation, but there was no room for negotiation here.

"Where's the studio?" New county heard from: Josh. Bobby was describing not only the location of the studio, but the route he was planning to take, as I ran upstairs to add protective layers to my ensemble.

"Have her home by ten," Daddy was hollering as we ducked out. "One minute later, the cops are there and you can say adios to the video thing—and to my money."

As it turned out, I was a little off in my guesstimate of the studio's population. When Bobby and I got there, I realized we were like, it. "Where is everybody?" I asked.

Bobby turned to me as he flipped the light switches on and smiled. "For rehearsing, we need the studio to ourselves. I figured you knew that and were just, uh, reassuring your old man?" Bobby peeled off his jacket and walked over to a CD player. He looked brutally hot.

I wanted to tell him about all the other workout tapes I'd surveyed and how I thought ours should be different, but Bobby tapped on his watch and said, "Let's get started, we've only got the studio for an hour and a half."

"I'm ready," I said. "You teach me, and then I'll show my friends."

Bobby put some way slow music on and began to talk softly. "I don't know how much you know about all this," he began, then looked at me appraisingly, "though you're clearly doing something right."

I blushed. "Well, it is important to keep in shape. That's why we're here, right? So we can teach everyone."

Just then Bobby's beeper went off. He looked annoyed when he checked the number. "Okay, so first thing—"

"Aren't you going to call whoever's beeping you?" I

asked, surprised. I mean, what if it was some famous celebrity?

"Later for that. Now, all the stuff we're gonna do is very strenuous, so we start with warm-ups."

"I'm feeling brutally warm already," I said, winking at him.

Bobby grinned. Baldwin to the max. "No, look, Cher. I'm serious. We've got lots of ground to cover in a very short time, that's why rehearsals are so crucial. Learn it right the first time and avoid injury."

"I totally understand," I said, flashing him my flirtiest smile. "But it's like that famous poem, right? No pain, no gain."

Bobby came way close to me, took my arm and gently raised it over my head, showing me how to stretch. "Just follow me and I promise, this will be absolutely painless."

For the next hour, Bobby demonstrated and I tried to follow. We stretched quads, biceps, triceps, glutes, hamstrings, and other strings I didn't know I had.

We marched. "To the left, step, one, two, to the right, step, three four . . ." Bobby drilled, over and over again until I got it right. We did body rolls, shoulder rolls, three-quarter neck rolls, arm curls, and way major flexing.

I was getting massively tired. The music Bobby had chosen was so wrong. It was like a boomerfest of Geritol journeymen. Which reminded me—I hadn't even told Bobby about Jesse. Or any of my other monster ideas, either.

"Bobby? Can we—ah—stop for a little while?" I was gasping for breath.

He looked concerned. "Are we overdoing it?"

"Not even," I breathed deeply. "Just wanted to give you the 411 on the contributions my friends and I are making."

"Contributions?" His look was way doubtful, but he said, "Sure. Okay." Bobby stopped the music and pulled up two folding chairs. He swung himself around to straddle one, folded his arms over the back, leaned in, and fixed me with a way intense gaze. Little tiny beads of sweat had formed on his bronzed forehead. His eyelashes were thick and dark—an amazing contrast to his light eyes. "Shoot, Cher. What's up?"

"Well, first of all, we've got some killer music," I started.

"Music already? You haven't seen all the exercises yet."

"Tscha! This music will go with everything. It's so dope."

"Cher, Cher," Bobby intoned, "I thought we agreed we're leaving the details to me and my people, remember?"

"We are," I agreed quickly, "Except this one. I mean, as a representative of my generation, I think I know what my peers will dance—I mean, work out—to. Besides, we can get the rights to this music for free, which will give us more budgetary resources for—"

Bobby slid his chair closer and grabbed my hands. "For free?" Now he was way excited. "You sure? How?"

"It's in the bag," I assured him. Then I explained about Jesse and his father. Bobby was hugely impressed. "In fact," I said brightly, "all my friends have rampantly important contributions. That's what's going to make this video the total bomb."

Bobby flashed a dazzling dental display. "Don't worry, Cher, no way it'll bomb. I'll see to that."

"Huh? Well, anyway, remember what you said about not wanting to shoot it in a studio?"

"I said that?" Bobby asked. I reminded him and sprung the Quad idea on him at the same time. He was less excited about that one. "I'll have to check that out first. You know, me and—"

"Your people?" I guessed.

He laughed. "How'd you get so cute, little Cher?"

"Umm, just comes naturally?" I answered. The "cute" part I liked, the "little Cher" part, not. Whatever. I continued, "And I'm thinking citrus—"

"Naturally. Fruit juices will be stocked at the bar," Bobby replied.

"No, silly! Citrus the fashion statement, not the beverage," I corrected him gently as I stared deeply into his astoundingly blue eyes. I rushed on, "I mean pastels are so 1995. And that black lycra stuff—positively Jurassic! Color is more than an accent, it's a focal point. The look in our video"—I paused to make sure he got the accent on *our*—"has to appeal to the generation I represent."

"Uh, generation X?" he guessed.

"*Hello?* We've all so had it up to here, with Generation X-traneous. This is for Generation A—as in acquisitive. The total picture has to appeal to us. The exercises are way important, but the ambience has to be there. I watched, like, bazillions of other videos and I see what they're missing."

"What they're missing, Cher"—Bobby reached out, covered my hands in his, and gazed at me way adoringly—"is us."

I swooned. I mean, I totally, absolutely, majorly, swooned.

If this were a movie, or even a cheesy movie of the week, this would have been the moment. I mean, there we were, all alone in this cavernous workout studio. Our lips were smolderingly close. And then Bobby got up and reached out to me. I closed my eyes. And waited.

Nothing happened. I tilted my head up and pursed my lips. Still nothing. I waited some more. Then I surreptitiously opened one eye.

That's when I saw Bobby standing over me, looking way confused. "Aren't you getting up?" he asked.

I wanted to scream, Aren't you going to kiss me?

Bobby leaned over to me and whispered. "Time for aerobics training. We haven't got the studio for much longer."

Bobby was fanatically determined to keep to our schedule. But what was I thinking, anyway? Bobby and I are business partners—for now. Later, basking in the glow of our video victory, that's when our relationship will progress. I so totally know that.

While I'd told Bobby I was thinking citrus, that was just preliminary. The shopping equivalent of warming up. It was time to get some real stretching—in a plastics sense—going. Which meant a fashion excursion into the cutting-edge world of designer workout gear. Okay, so I'm not all that sure to what extent that actually exists, but call me mental, I'm determined to find out.

Normally, I speed shop the Beverly Center, but today I couldn't. I'm shopping for my entire generation. Like, what good are killer abs without killer ensembles? And then there's the makeup aspect. That's got to be rampantly right, too.

I shopped everywhere. I surveyed, I inventoried. I even asked smarmy salespeople for help. There was the usual, "been there, done that, bought the T-shirt" stuff, Adidas, Champion, Danskin, Nike, Reebok, blah, blah, blech. Still, just to be sure, I convinced salespeople at each stop to give me one sample outfit for free. I promised each one a credit line at the end of the video, you know, "Outfits by" if they were actually used.

I stopped at the MAC makeup store, where I usually buy stuff. As I snagged some free samples there, I was really thinking we needed a personal makeup pro during the shoot. I whipped out my cellular and got the number for François Nars. He's so totally happening now. I left a message.

Boldly, I trekked on. I notched up what passes for fitness fashion from Liz Claiborne, Hot Skins, Fila, Mossimo, and Marika. Perry Ellis, Lauren's Polo Sport, and DKNY Tech had the boy market covered, designer-wise, so I picked up a couple of elastic-waist shorts and tanks ensembles from each in Bobby's size.

I was getting closer, but the colors were so not happening. Where were the lemons? The grapefruits? The oranges? The tangerines?

And where was Armani? Versace? Gucci? And I mean, hello? Calvin totally does lingerie, but what about workout stuff? Has he missed the powerboat here? And then it hit me—what if I ordered some stuff that wasn't originally meant as workout gear, but was so classic, it could totally do the job? Righteous.

By the time I got home, it was way late, and I'd promised like twenty different salespeople a credit line at the end of the video. I went up to my room and dumped all the outfits on the floor. Whew! The pile was major high. I was listening to the randoms on my voice messaging service when Lucy arrived with my dinner tray.

"Thanks, Luce. I am so ragged."

"What's all this?" she asked, pointing to the piles.

"Possible outfits for my exercise video."

"You are going to wear them all?" she asked incredulously.

"Tscha, Luce! They're just samples. I'm trying them on, deciding what's best for my generation."

It was half past *ER*, and George Clooney was locking lips with the guest star of the week, when I finally got started on my homework. It was way into *Letterman* by the time I realized I hadn't even eyeballed the files with Zinger records. I muted Dave, grabbed a highlighter, and started.

I don't know when Lucy came in to shut off the light.

# Chapter 9

I went into total shopping overdrive. Once I'd discarded the idea of using actual workout gear, an entire new world of possibilities opened up. I stepped forth bravely. Amber often tagged along. She is so into being seen with me. She figures that an alliance with me will totally boost her election chances.

Of course, Amber has less chance of being elected than I do of being seen in something off the rack. But I had to give her snaps for persistence. Okay, so her campaign speeches were majorly cheesy—not to mention those pathetic posters lining the halls of our school. In one effort, her team had painted Elect Honest Amber under her photo. If that alone wasn't bad enough, some random had crossed out the *M* and the *R* and crudely drawn a black stovepipe hat and beard on it. The poster now read, Elect Honest ABE. I'd never realized the resemblance between Amber and our sixteenth prez before. Even so, it was way harsh. I ripped it down before Amber could see it.

Besides, even though Amber was off on her campaign swing, she was the one who showed up most consistently at rehearsals. Bobby never seemed too thrilled to see her. While he and his people had scouted the Quad and approved its use for the location, he brutally rebuffed Amber's idea of using "her constituents"—the sophomore class—as dancers in the video, explaining that we needed professionals. Someone else might have been crushed, but not Amber. For better or worse, the girl is majorly resilient.

Buff Bobby focused on teaching us the routines. Our warm-ups included lots of deep breathing, stretches, biceps and triceps curls, marches, and pliés. It was easier since Jesse had supplied the actual music, and Bobby redesigned the exercises to go along with it. He'd even worked in "Exhale (Shoop Shoop)" and "Sittin' Up in My Room." De will so totally kvell. If she ever manages time for a rehearsal. So far it's rehearsals-10; De-0.

I mean, Murray, Sean, and Jesse were all majorly busy, but they'd cameoed at the studio sporadically. Surprisingly, De's new friends, Shaniqua, Shawana, and Essence, were nearly up to speed rehearsal-wise, too. Even Tai managed to show up once or twice, albeit with the drooling dog in tow. "It's good training for Peabo to be with people," Tai had said brightly. She'd dressed him up for his big outing in a terry cloth bandanna. When I suggested DKNY makes a classier ascot, Tai confided that Peabo drooled so much, she needed something more absorbent under his neck. But Peabo didn't get a chance to train with people, because Buff Bobby insisted that Tai keep "that creature" outside. Which totally cut into Tai's concentration on the exercise routines.

In the aerobics portion, we learned the knee to elbow crossover, the squat with shoulder press, the kick across, and a whole bunch of lunges. I couldn't help but be majorly mesmerized by Buff Bobby. Like, before I met him? I'd never heard the expression "washboard abs." I never even knew what a washboard was. But Bobby really *was* all that—and a double latte.

"Left, right, step up, step together." Bobby was demonstrating. "Back, back, back, and kick—press, squeeze your butt, press, and squeeze."

"Let's bring those arms up," Bobby instructed. "And keep the feet down, just the body moves, bring the right leg in, six, seven, eight. Pull it up, that's right."

Bobby was juiced as he watched us. "Yes! The leg keeps lifting. Let's march it out; let's punch it out, five, six, seven, pump it out. Let's pick it up—bend those knees, Cher!"

Bobby's body moved to the rhythm way righteously as he sang out, "Hands behind the hips, here we go. Keep moving in place, add a turn, back it up, march it out, step right, step back, step left, and turn. Here we go, five, six, seven . . . "

Bobby was majorly patient with us, even when we misstepped or our beepers went off in the middle of the routines. He seemed to understand that just because he kept ignoring *his* beeper didn't mean I could do the same. Daddy was still into keeping major tabs on me.

I couldn't understand why Bobby never seemed overly thrilled with my friends and always, like, stuck them behind me. The only thing that sent him really ballistic, though, was when Amber's jewelry jangled or got in the way. Tolerating Amber, I could see, didn't come naturally to Bobby. But then again, that took special talent.

All in all, I had to totally back-pat myself for the way things were going. We were so making our way toward glorious glutes, tauter tummies, and tonier triceps. Feeling the burn and bringing my t.b.'s together, while benefiting teenkind at the same time. All my friends were not only psyched, but making valuable contributions. With the glaring exception of De. And now there was the Murray dumping thing to deal with. Two situations that had totally vaulted to the top of the intervention-priority list.

I determined to corner De for a major confession session. I had to make her see how her wholesale dumping was so negatively affecting her formerly near and dear. Still, I wanted to present my grievances in a rational way. A way that showed I could be supportive and understanding but still get my point across. I didn't want to alienate De any further. Which is why I totally was not prepared to fly off the handle the way I did the next day in the hallway outside Geist's class.

But there was De, all two-toned mocha silk chiffon

crop top, matching A-line skirt and way cheesy waist beads, going, "Sure, let's make it Tuesday afternoon, I'm free."

I can't decide which set me off, the fact that she was carelessly breaking a rehearsal date *again* or that she was currently interfacing with Ohagi, a brutally gorgeous African-American Baldwin. Whichever, in a move totally worthy of Amber, I viciously elbowed my way into their conversation pit.

"Excuse me, *girlfriend,"* I said sarcastically, "but if I'm not mistaken, the Tuesday slot on your dance card is already filled."

De turned to me, way confused. "Huh?"

I enlightened her. "Rehearsal, De? A word that seems to be missing from your vocabulary list. And if you don't like that one, try another. Friendship. Hello? Remember that one?" I was majorly feeling the burn now, and it wasn't from hitting the exercise wall.

De gave me a strange look. It was like she was trying to match my heightened emotional state but wasn't sure why. Ohagi broke in, "Uh, I think I'd better go, De. I'll buzz you later."

De waved him away distractedly. She was probably about to apologize to me, but I didn't give her the chance. Weeks of frustration spewed forth.

"I can't believe you, De. We're supposed to be doing the exercise video. You and me, together. You *committed* to this. You tell me, like, 'Oh, I always dreamed of leading a workout tape,' and now that I've made it happen, you're never there. Does your journey mean you suddenly stop honoring commitments? Do we from your old journey not count anymore?" I stopped for a breath, but not long enough for De to get a word in. "You're not only turning your back on me, you're betraying all of teenage America," I finished with a flourish.

Finally, De cut in, "Chill, Cher! I haven't betrayed anyone. I don't even know all of teenage America. Get a grip!"

I was still majorly flustered, "Well, how could you tell that—that—Ohagi dude you're free on Tuesday? Rehearsals are Tuesday. Of course, you wouldn't know that from personal experience, but I have left repeated messages on your answering machine. And once upon a time, you did promise to show up."

"You know, Cher, if you'd cut the sarcasm, we can actually discuss this."

The bell rang for next period, but I wasn't close to the finish line. Just then Mrs. Gardner, the vice principal, appeared. In a flat voice, she said, "Take it somewhere else, ladies. If you don't have a class to be in, I suggest you go outside."

I grabbed De's elbow and headed into the girls room. Amber's campaign poster, with the slogan "Free us from a slavish elective system," did little for the general ambience. Still, at least the stalls were empty.

"I don't really know what's got your Calvins out of joint," De began, as soon as the door swung closed behind us, "Okay, so that rehearsal thing might have slipped my mind momentarily—"

"Oh, and did the fact that you have a boyfriend also slip your mind momentarily?" I said snidely. Oops—how did that come out? I haven't even figured out a plan for bringing De and Murray back together.

De leaned back on the sink. She folded her arms in front of her chest and took a deep breath.

"Okay, Cher, here's the 411. I'll ride the shame spiral about the rehearsal thing. You're right. I did make a commitment. But you are totally out of line to bring up Murray. You have no idea where I am in terms of that."

"De, I have no idea where you are, period."

"Then allow me clue you in now. That is, if you think you can listen without going postal. You might even find something to mull in that boy-obsessed brain of yours."

Boy obsessed? As if!

"Over the past weeks, I've come to some life-changing realizations," De began.

I slid my Tignianello backpack off my shoulder and let it drop on the floor and leaned against Amber's poster. It sounded like De was about to deliver some major crushing blow from which I needed to be cushioned.

"One of which is this. We've all been raised in a society where we think we need a boyfriend or we don't count. If we're not attached to the male of the species, we're nothing. We have no self-esteem."

I was about to say how I so totally did not agree with that, but De was on a roll.

"And what I've realized, being with my sisters, is how bogus that is. We are strong, independent young women. We have worth, we have value, we can do anything, be anything, dress any way we want. We don't need to impress men. We do not need men to define who we are and who we can be."

"De, if you could just climb down off your soapbox for a second—"

She couldn't. "Our overreliance on men isn't even fair to them, because we're just using boys to make us feel good about ourselves."

"De, aren't you like, leaving out something here?"

"I don't think so, Cher."

"What about love? What about the fact that Murray has been sprung on you forever, and like he'd do anything for you. Doesn't your journey take you to that place? And besides, Murray is the flyest boy at school."

"Well, you know what? It's time for him to fly away. I've cut him loose, given Murray his wings, Cher."

"Why, so you can hook up with Ohagi? If you don't need a man, why were you making a date with him?" I demanded.

"A date? You really have lost it, Cher. Ohagi's in my science class. He's my lab partner, and we had to find some time to write up our report."

Oops.

"Which leads me to you, Cher. Every time you see two people of the opposite sex together, you assume they either want to be romantically linked or should be."

"Me? I don't even have a boyfriend."

"But you'd like one. And I am speaking of that ambition-plagued, stardom-obsessed, surgically enhanced Buff Bobby of yours." De stared at me levelly.

"He's not surgically enhanced! Every ounce of his fat-free body has been shaped, toned, and flexed by exercise." Okay, that was lame, but it was all I could manage. De had so totally blindsided me.

"Every ounce of his body is devoted to self-promotion, Cher. Not to making the world safer for tubby teenagers, and certainly not because he has any real interest in you."

"And by what powers of deduction did you come to that conclusion, De? You only met him once."

"Once was enough. He's only using you to make money—and to make himself look good."

"Not even, De! Just because you're all cynical now—"

But De had started for the door. "You don't need him, Cher, but he needs you. For now."

I should have gone righteously postal. But that wasn't the emotion that washed to the surface. Instead, I felt disconnected and lonelier than ever. De and I used to be best friends. And I'm actually okay with the fact that she has other friends now, too. But what did I do to deserve being deserted? And what did I do to deserve this blast from her?

De's final, "I might not be at the next rehearsal, but I'm a fast learner and I'll be there when you need me," rang in my ears as she sashayed out of the girls room. Amber's poster eyes followed her.

I didn't get to say, "I miss our friendship. I miss you, De."

De didn't show up at the next rehearsal. But her spirit was there. She'd given me plenty to think about. While there might have been a thread of truth in the who-needs-boys oral, she was significantly wrong about Bobby. And she was totally boneheaded about her and Murray. They so belong together.

In a weird way, it was De's passion that finally gave me an idea for making that happen. De and Murray express their love by fighting. If they had something to fight about, would they not be back together? I remembered that famous quote: "Necessity is the mother of invention." Since it was totally necessary that De and Murray get back together, I decided to invent something for them to fight about. Something that would jolt De back into the reality zone and make her see how much she totally loves Murray.

It was during rehearsal that it hit me. Brainstorm.

"Bobby, can we put this on pause for a sec? I have an urgent phone call to make."

Bobby seemed a little miffed. He checked his faux Rolex and said, "Make it quick, okay?" Then he grabbed a towel and headed over to the juice machine.

I dug my cellular out of my backpack and punched in Murray's number.

"Murray? Check it. You're going out for the football team."

"Cher? Have you totally lost it? I'm not down with football, girl. I don't play the game. A brother could get hurt out there."

"Tscha, Murray. You're not really gonna play it. Just tell Sean you're signing up. That way, the word will be spread around the entire school by tomorrow. And when De finds out—"

"De! She'd go crazy if she thought I was goin' out for football."

"Precisely." I hung up and went back to my reps. Bobby was waiting.

I was starting to feel way optimistic again. I was

totally secure that my plan for bringing De and Murray back together was foolproof. And I was making great strides on the fashion front. After going through a veritable alphabet of bodywear—Adidas, Aerodynamics, BUM, Baryshnikov, Carushka, Danskin, Expozay, Fila, etc., I finally settled on the ensembles we'd wear in the video. It took me to *T.* Some random company called Trixi had actually invented something totally different and rampantly now.

It was a shiny patent zip-front bustier top, paired with mini nylon and patent vinyl skirt. But since we can't work out in a skirt, I'd change that to shorts. And the color it came in—black—to shades of citrus. Then I thought, studs on the bustier would add that extra dash of our generation chic.

The manufacturers reps were way open to the adjustments. Especially after I ordered several dozen ensembles in a variety of sizes and mentioned price not being an object and all.

For the boys, I decided to go all the way with DKNY Tech. For Bobby, who'd be side by side with me in the video, I went with sky blue to match his eyes.

If there was a fly in my satisfaction ointment—besides De, that is—it was Josh. Who'd—hello?—worn out his welcome weeks ago, but inexplicably was still around. And of course I'd promised to keep him in the progress-loop. I made the best of it by getting him to drive me places. But we always argued. LIke the day before, Josh was chauffeuring me to rehearsal and I was extolling Bobby's various virtues.

"I wish you'd show a little more passion for things

that matter, instead of that dimwit exercise guy" was all Josh could manage.

"Bobby does matter," I said stubbornly. "I don't know what you have against him or our project."

"Tell me something, Cher. What exactly is he doing? You and your friends are demonstrating the exercises. Your friends procured the music, the location, and the distribution. You're getting the outfits."

"That just shows how little you know, Josh. Bobby's people are handling the details. Bobby's, like, the engineer, the creative designer of the whole package. We're partners. Of course, I'm doing stuff, but so is he. He's taking care of way important stuff."

"I'll just bet he is," Josh said snidely.

When we reached the studio, I tried to dart out of the car before Josh could say anything else. But I wasn't fast enough. "By the way, Cher, how're you doing on the Zinger depo?"

Uh-oh. Josh had zoned in on the one thing I might have let slip.

"Great. Right on time," I totally lied. Not only had I not worked on it lately, I wasn't sure I could locate it if I had to. But it was somewhere in my room.

As I dashed into the studio, I made a mental note to dig it up that night. And work on it.

Only by the time I got home, my mental capacities were as diminished as my musculature. I was one massive achy, breaky ball of sweat. My room looked like the junior department at Saks after a one-day sale. All the sample outfits I'd gone through were strewn around the room in piles once divided by styles, colors, and appropriateness. Of course, now that I'd chosen the actual outfits, I didn't need these anymore. Only I didn't have the stamina to even think about putting anything away. I buzzed Lucy on the intercom.

"Ya, Cher?" came her familiar voice.

It was late and I didn't want to bug Lucy with anything major, so I just said, "Sometime tomorrow—or whenever—could you like deal with this pile of clothes on my floor?"

"How should I deal with them? You want them in your closet?"

I didn't. "Um, do you know anyone who might want them, Lucy? They're like, samples of outfits I'm not using in the video."

"I have to think about it, Cher. But I'll clean it up off your floor tomorrow."

"Thanks, Luce, I totally appreciate it."

I fell asleep, dreaming of "step to the left, step to the right." The Zinger depo did not appear in my dreams or anywhere else.

# Chapter 10

The last two weeks before the actual video shoot were way intense. The rehearsal schedule escalated to every other day after school, often spilling over into the nights. Weekends were not spared. Bobby drilled the routines into us—okay, those of us who were there. He introduced us to the director, one Harry Haverford, straight out of central casting: about five feet, four inches, pony tail, dangling modifier, baseball cap. At first, I wasn't sure what we needed Harry for. "I thought you were the director, Bobby," I said.

"Talented as I am"—Bobby winked—"even I can't be two places at once, and my place is on camera—next to you."

On the up side, De finally showed up for rehearsal and after a couple of sessions, capably mastered the routines. I'd forgotten what a quick learner she was.

Not to mention De hadn't let herself go. Regardless of her anti-boy rhetoric, her abs were still totally fab. I had to give her snaps for that.

Best of all, I'd scored the ultimate makeup coup. After a battery of calls—like from all my afternoon classes for days—I'd finally gotten through to a human in François Nars's studio. Okay, so I couldn't convince François himself to do the job. As if being on call for one Sharon Stone movie is more important than our video—like, hello? Who's got the longer shelf life here? I did engage one of his assistants, Tony somebody-or-other, who, I was assured, was totally trained by François, used the same products and did the same job, only cheaper.

On the down side, Bobby had unilaterally vetoed my suggestions to add a nutritional segment to the video. I tried to explain how restaurant and take-out tips would be way relatable to our generation, but Bobby was all, "My people hired writers, just follow the script, Cher. We don't have time for your additions."

But by the time I scanned the script, which Buff Bobby's people didn't deliver until like, just before the shoot, I realized how lame it was. As if I'd ever say, "I love exercise, because it puts you in touch with your body." That had to go. I also realized how much was missing. So I added stuff.

I chalked Bobby's crankiness up to nerves. Way understandable, under the circumstances. Bobby's people were giving him grief, and he'd started to mention some benefactress named Marlene who was complaining. I took it that the old hag had been the one beeping him constantly. "Marlene doesn't like any of the titles for the video" was the missive Buff Bobby left on my voice messaging service.

That was another issue. After powwowing with my friends, we'd come up with a whole bunch of viable titles. We'd submitted "The Totally Golden Betty & Baldwin Workout," "Extreme Fitness with Cher Horowitz & Friends," "The Total Teen Mind & Body Makeover," "Power Shaping the Cher Way," and the short but sweet "Sweat."

In the end, we went with "Fitbuzz: The Ultimate Body Tune-up for Teens, by Bobby Van Hoosen with Cher Horowitz."

We'd been working so hard that all vestiges of fun, in a social-life sense, had virtually vanished. Jesse complained bitterly about how a late-running rehearsal had kept us from a party in Bel Air.

"I figured you and me could make that scene, together, Cher," he'd said smarmily, coming up behind me and massaging my neck. Which felt good, but going to a party as Jesse's date? When pigs fly.

Yet Jesse's bellyaching gave me an idea. What if we had our own party to kick off the video, a good-luck fiesta the night before the shoot? It would totally loosen everyone up, especially Buff Bobby, who was in need of an industrial strength chill pill. We'd all go into the video shoot the next day feeling properly pumped. Besides, the workout ensembles had arrived yesterday and were majorly the bomb. I could not wait to distribute them to one and all. The party was the perfect place.

But when I laid the idea on Bobby, he was reluctant to commit. "A party? Uhm, I don't know, Cher. It doesn't sound like a great idea. What if people get, uh, too tired, or trashed or something?"

"Not even, Bobby, just the opposite. A social gathering will bring us all together. We'll feel like a team going into this. Besides, I know someone who could use a little loosening up."

With that, I reached up and gently chucked him under his square, massively smooth chin.

"Stress shows, huh, Cher?" Buff Bobby said guiltily.

"Like Amber's visible panty lines," I said. Then, I got another idea. "Plus, I've got the primo party place—my own backyard! No one would dare get trashed there."

Unlike Buff Bobby, my friends were way NNE—as in Need No Encouragement. They gave the party idea a rousing thumbs up and agreed to spread the word around school. I alerted Lucy and Jose, our groundskeeper, made a few catering and decorating calls, and within a few hours, it was all set for the Friday night before the shoot.

Daddy was going to be off on a business trip, but no way would I do this behind his back. I *had* to ask permission. *He* had to assign a baby-sitter, namely, Josh. "It's not that I don't trust you and your friends, Cher," Daddy said as I packed his overnight case, "but you never know what can happen, and Josh is sensible. He always has a level head."

Since the video was happening on Saturday, Bobby had scheduled dress rehearsal—a major misnomer since I hadn't even distributed the ensembles yet—for the Thursday before. The school administration had graciously agreed to cancel afternoon classes because of it, which sent the entire population into major spasms of applause for me.

Bobby and his crew arrived in the morning in trailers and vans. It took them, like, hours to unload the huge klieg-light contraptions, cameras, cables, a righteous CD player, and audio boards riddled with control panels. A plethora of baseball-capped randoms, massively wired with beepers and walkie-talkies, sprouted up everywhere. Some carried scripts. Briefly, I considered clueing them in to the changes I'd made, but I figured they probably expected me to ad-lib. I'm pretty sure Amber Valletta and Shalom Harlow do on *House of Style*.

Bobby and director-dude Harry were huddled together when I ducked out of Hall's class to officially welcome them to the Quad.

"Zup, Bobby," I greeted him cheerily.

He frowned when he saw me. "That's not what you're gonna wear?"

I was in my school clothes, an Anna Molinari supersoft sleeveless leather top draped at the neck, a Celine barely there mini, and Ferragamo sandals.

"Duh, Bobby, of course not. But I couldn't very well wear a workout ensemble to school. I'll change when we're ready. Stop stressing."

But Bobby had already stopped. He turned his attention back to Harry and the crew, pointing out where stuff should go. Bobby is the most majorly directed Baldwin I have ever met. I'm surprised Daddy didn't see that quality in him.

Later Bobby's professional dancers arrived. A jumble of about a dozen dudes and dudettes with massive muscle definition going on. They all lounged around the Quad in their generic workout suits, sipping fruit juices and Evian as if they were, like, in Hawaii, or something. One dudette in particular, all spindly long legs, wavy auburn hair, and overly mascaraed green eyes, kept sidling up to Bobby, whispering in his ear. Mostly, he ignored her.

"Places! Places, everyone!" Director Harry was clamoring for order. He actually had a bullhorn, which Sean found wildly amusing. "Yo, I could use that for pagin' the posse," he yelled. A comment that went underappreciated by Bobby. He helped intersperse his dancers among my friends. Murray, Sean, Tai, and Jesse were way in the back row, while Shawana, Shaniqua, Essence, De, and Amber were scrunched in the middle. Bobby had placed two of his dancers for each of my friends. If I hadn't known better, I'd have thought he was trying to camouflage them. Naturally, Bobby and I were out front.

"Let's hold for lighting," one of the wired randoms—later, I found out they were mostly AD's, assistant directors—shouted. Then a deejay dude started the music. But he only let Mary J. Blige do a few bars of "Not Gon' Cry," before the sound engineer, removing his headphones, gave the signal to stop.

"Okay, Cher, you can start your narration now." Harry instructed me to read a few bars from the script.

I started, but before I got a full sentence out, was brutally silenced. "That's enough," Harry said. "We just need to hear your voice to adjust the volume levels."

And that's how the afternoon went. We'd start doing something, only to be stopped for one tech reason after another. We'd start, we'd stop, like a zillion and one times. Who could blame us for getting way bored? It was just like class.

So, during the interminable waits, it was only natural that beepers went off, cellulars were whipped out, teeth flossed, and sidebars flourished. All of which wigged out Harry, Bobby, and company, but after a while, even they gave up trying to get us to, like stand still or something. Besides, their attention was way diverted by matters majorly technical.

Murray, who came to rehearsal in a football jersey, kept trying to talk jock talk—as long as De was in audio range. At one point, he shouted, "Yeah, I'm aimin' to go out for that touchdown position." I reminded him that touchdown wasn't a position.

"I see you more as a tight end," Shaniqua giggled, pointing to Murray's butt.

De ignored the banter. She and Essence practiced routines.

Murray kept trying. He turned to Amber. "Now that I'm gonna be a jock, I guess I can't vote for you, Amber. My posse on the football team's all for your opponent."

"Traitor!" Amber screamed. Either she hadn't been clued in to the fact that Murray was just posing as jock, or she was a better actress than I gave her credit for.

"Can't help it," Murray said loudly, looking straight

at De. "All us *jocks* are goin' with Brian Fuller and I gotta be a team player."

"Places, dancers!" Harry was at the bullhorn again, interrupting Murray's little playact.

"Action!" Harry commanded.

It was way late when Bobby and his crew packed up to leave. My friends and I were more ragged from boredom than actual fatigue. As I headed into the lockers to change, I realized how critical tomorrow night's party would be. After today, we all needed a spirit infusion.

I was just punching in the number of the caterer to check on the hors d'oeuvres, when Amber, Tai, and Shawana strolled over purposefully. I suddenly felt cornered.

"Cher," Tai began, all innocent, "don't take this the wrong way, but—"

Uh-oh. I hoped this wasn't about the video.

"Well, you would be the first to tell us if things were like, the other way around," she continued.

"What things? What way around? Cut to the chase, Tai."

Amber did the cutting. "We *have* to be honest. And we all agree that Bobby is wrong for you."

They all agree? I was buggin'. "Well, thanks for sharing, girlfriends, but I don't remember soliciting your opinions." I turned to finish getting dressed.

"He's radically cute, Cher," Tai admitted, "but he's too old for you."

"Not even," I countered, wondering why I was letting myself be drawn into this debate. "Bobby's more evolved than the single-celled amoebas here at school, but he's majorly in his prime—in case you hadn't noticed."

Shawana chimed in, "I'm not tryin' to get in your business, Cher, but that Himbo is not for you."

And when had the distaff side of TLC decided she could give me advice?

"Yeah, Cher, it's like De says—"

De! So *that's* what this is about.

I turned to Tai, and in a language she could understand, I said, "I'm muting you."

Amber, however, would not be muted. "Bobby's not even in our universe. What could you have in common with him? Fashionally speaking. Like, have you ever seen him out of exercise gear?"

I flashed on Bobby's perfect physique and killer abs. I had to smile. "Doy, Amber, why would I want to?"

The next day, I took off from school. I needed to supervise the party preparations and get in shape for the big day. I scheduled the manicurist, aromatherapist, and an extra hour with Fabianne, who was majorly thrilled at what her original suggestion had wrought. "It seems like forever ago that you hooked me up with Buff Bobby, doesn't it, Fabianne?" I'd said, and invited her to the next day's shoot.

In between and during my appointments, I fielded phone calls.

Everything was on track. Spago was delivering brick-oven salmon pizza, and I'd chosen Zuma Sushi, in honor of my first meeting with Bobby, to do the hors d'oeuvres.

Murray buzzed to say that he and his father had nailed two distributors for the video. Providing, of course, we delivered on time. "Tscha! Not to worry, Murray," I assured him. "Everything's happening. Like, what could go wrong?"

"That's what I told the Blockbuster reps," Murray said enthusiastically. "I told them you were down with the timing and all."

"Any progress on the De front?" I asked before hanging up.

"Not yet, but I'm feeling pretty positive that's gonna turn around, too."

I was feeling way positive myself when Bobby called. He said it was to "flesh out and firm up" the timing for tomorrow. But I knew he just wanted an excuse to hear my voice.

"I'm feeling pretty firm, Bobby, thanks to you, that is." I giggled. Bobby was so cute when he was all nervous. We talked timing a little, then I said, "I'll see you tonight. Oh, and Bobby, you did invite your dancers to come?"

"Uh, no, I didn't think it was necessary," he answered, clicking off.

Friday night arrived all balmy and breezy. I went outside to survey the pool area before anyone arrived. I had to give Jose and the decorators major snaps for the Hall of Fame job they'd done on seriously short notice. The lighting was soft and affirmative. The fountains were in full sprinkler mode and the Claes Oldenburg sculptures sparkled in the high beams.

Tuxedoed waiters set up stations of sushi, personal pizzas, and assorted finger food. The bar was stocked with Arizona Iced Tea, Snapple, designer water, and carbonated drinks, too. Little cocktail tables, imported for the night, dotted the pool area, and Jose had turned on the outdoor speakers so music could flow as freely as the Snapple.

Although supervision is my strong suit, this time I got hands-on involved. I created a multicolored banner from my computer's Print Shop program that read Good Luck, Team Video!

I was feeling majorly fabulous as I went upstairs to dress for the evening. I flipped on the computer and went to my personal fashion home page: http://www.romantic dress/no boyfriend.com.

A whole bunch of suggestions came up on the screen. Among my choices were a backless Calvin, a shimmery Prada, a sequined Badgley Mischka, and a velvet pastel Chanel party dress. I went with the last, mainly because it was cloudless sky blue. Like Bobby's eyes.

Final touch: an emotion potion. I spritzed Chanel's Allure all over my bedroom and did a few laps through the spray. I checked the full-length. Proper.

Amber was the first to arrive. A good thing, too, because I needed the extra time to recover from her outfit. My guess? Because she inexplicably assumed Ferrari Fred was going to be there, she went all out. She tried hard to look like *a* real babe, only she missed and ended up as *the* real Babe. Pink and furry all over, from her angora top to her short-haired, I mean, nubby little faux-Chanel skirt. She'd topped it off with a way ridiculous headband and bottomed out with fringed pink patent leather boots. She even had a leather choker with a silver dogtag. Way porcine.

My jaw dropped. It even appeared her snout—I mean, nose—had been surgically enhanced for the evening.

"What's the matter, Cher? Can't deal with a little fashion competition?" she grunted.

"Yeah, right, Amber. That must be it." I turned away and headed over to the bar.

Invitees began to arrive. Soon the cobblestoned circular was riddled with Jeeps, BMWs, Lexuses, and limos. I hadn't seen Bobby's Stealth when I first checked, but later, when I turned around after giving Essence and Tai their video ensembles, there he was. Like a vision.

It was the first time I'd seen Buff Bobby out of exercise gear. He was way Brad Pitt at the Oscars, dark jacket with white, wide-collared, open-neck shirt. It didn't appear to be from any of the important designers, but Bobby still looked fierce. I could do wonders with him at the Tommy Hilfiger boutique, I calculated, or at Hugo Boss. In fact, once the video was out and we were on the publicity trail promoting it, Bobby's wardrobe makeover would be priority one.

I sidled up to him.

"Cher!" He greeted me in his usual, but his tone was a little lacking in confidence. Bobby was slightly out of his element and probably still uptight about tomorrow. "You look . . . different," he said, in full appreciation mode.

"Ditto," I said, getting up close and personal. "And your cologne is majorly macho."

We interfaced. I was nervous, so I babbled about insignificant stuff. But Buff Bobby was massively engrossed in everything I had to say. Not that he added much. It hit me that if we weren't discussing the video, Bobby wasn't much of a conversationalist. But I didn't dwell on that.

Just then I saw Murray. He was wearing a football jersey and sweatpants. They totally clashed with his DKNY loafers. I was about to walk over to him when Bobby said, "Would you—uh—want to dance?"

I didn't hesitate. I wrapped my arms around Bobby's neck, and he pulled me close.

And that's how I knew.

Everyone else was wrong and I was right. Maybe Bobby hadn't said so in exact words, and maybe he'd missed, like, a zillion opportunities to kiss me, but at that moment, wrapped in his way developed arms, I totally knew that he was feeling what I was feeling.

Of course Bobby had been totally focused on the job he had to do. I mean, the job *we* had to do. He felt totally responsible for the video and for helping all of teendom to benefit from his expertise. What had I expected? That he'd compromise his professional standards for personal reasons? No matter how strongly he felt about me, Bobby hadn't let those feelings interfere with his work.

But after tomorrow? When the video is wrapped?

That was when he'd show me his real feelings. That was when our business relationship would expand into a more personal arena. Look at him. Buff Bobby was so the reason I don't date high school boys. He was everything I'd been searching for in the boyfriend department. We were so meant for each other. Like Madonna and Carlos—wasn't he her trainer first? And Julia Roberts—she was dating her fitness guru, too. It was way cutting-edge kismet. Or something.

One song ended and another began. At least I thought so. Encircled in Buff Bobby's massive arms, my head nestling on his chest, I was totally in another time zone. I barely registered seeing Josh, leaning against the bar, surveying the scene. I did notice what he was wearing—that disapproving big-brother look.

I closed my eyes and let Buff Bobby lead me. He was a way smooth dancer, but then again, physical stuff is his forte. Suddenly, something crashed into my reverie. It took a moment to focus and realize it was Amber—looking for Ferrari Fred.

"I invited him," she wailed. "I can't believe he didn't show up. Did he call?"

I turned my head the other way and tuned her out. In my field of vision on the other side, I saw something majorly heartwarming. "Oh, look at that," I said to Bobby, pointing toward the tennis courts. "It's Sean, dancing with Shawana. Look how he's looking into her eyes. He's totally sprung on her. He's in full-tilt worship mode. Isn't that sweet?"

Bobby didn't respond, but when the slow dance was over, he held on to me a little longer than required.

Then he released me from his grip and said, "In honor of our video, I brought something for you."

Bobby got me a gift? That was so rampantly meaningful! He pulled a small bag out of his pocket and offered it to me. "Go ahead, look inside," he urged.

I couldn't imagine what it was. Jewelry? But there was no, like Tiffany box or anything. And it wasn't wrapped. I opened the bag and peeked inside.

It turned out to be something even better than jewelry. Something that came from Bobby's heart. And way appropriate under the circumstances.

It was a black Nike headband. "It's to wear tomorrow at the shoot," Bobby said bashfully.

How sweet! But how could I tell him it would totally clash with my outfit? No, I had to pretend to love it. As much as I loved him.

"Oh, Bobby, that's so—" I was about to thank him in a meaningful way, when we were brutally interrupted. Jesse inflicted himself upon us.

"There you are! I've been looking all over for you, Cher." Jesse's timing couldn't have been worse, but still, I had to give him snaps for his fashion sense. He was all Istante pants, V-necked sweater, and logo blazer, accessorized with J. P. Tod pebble-soled moccasins.

Jesse was cradling a stack of CDs in one arm. With the other, he grabbed me around the waist and nuzzled my neck. "Hmm, you smell ripe," he murmured.

Under normal circumstances, I would have forcefully removed all traces of Jesse from my personal space, but until the video was complete, I needed him and his music on my good side. So as gently as possible, I disentangled myself.

"New music?" I said, pointing to his CDs. "Why don't you take them over to Jose and ask him to play them?"

But Jesse wouldn't be dismissed that easily. I had to dance with him first. I kept sneaking glances at Buff Bobby the whole time.

What finally freed me from Jesse's unwanted attention was a commotion of major proportions over by the deep end of the pool. Two people were arguing. And things were escalating way quickly. Voices were raised. Finger food was being thrown.

It was music to my ears. I ran up to bear witness.

"So what's all this with the stupid-ass football follies, Murray?" De was doing demanding as only De can do.

"No follies, Miss Dionne." Murray got into the denial groove swiftly. "I'm goin' out for that three-quarter back position." With that, Murray pantomimed a faux-football pass.

De eyed him suspiciously and started to raise her voice. "You never cared about school sports before. What's this sudden change of 'tude about?"

"I got more time on my hands now, but I guess you know that. Besides, what's it to you? Now that you're all *empowered* and stuff. Whatchoo care about what I do?" Murray began to match her, decibel for decibel.

"I don't!" De huffed, and turned on her heel. But suddenly, her real emotions got the better of her. She whirled around, picked a California roll off a passing tray, and threw it at him, shrieking, "Where are your brains, idiot-boy? You'll break your neck! You'll break your leg! You'll break your braces!"

Murray grabbed a slice of salmon off his personal pie and lobbed it at her. He missed, but it was enough to start a full-out food fight. Everyone at the party grabbed food. Hors d'oeuvres soon made graceful arcs through the air. Cheese flew off the brick-oven pizza slices.

Just as in the old days, people took sides. Mostly the girls took De's side, while the boys were behind Murray. Unfortunately, they weren't directly behind him. The pool was. And as De and her all-girl posse advanced on him, Murray took one step too many backward. Out of the corner of my eye, I saw Josh, on his way to intervene. He wasn't fast enough.

"Ahaahhh!" was the last sound I heard before some extremely major splashing, accompanied by random screams of "My suede shoes got wet!" and "My hair's trashed!'" from various members of the assembled.

And then, above the gurgling and splashing, we all heard, "Hold on, bro. I'll save you!" Sean didn't even take his Air Jordans off before diving in after Murray.

Buff Bobby was suddenly at my side. He was appalled. "What are they doing? The shoot's tomorrow!"

I slipped my arm around Buff Bobby's waist and snuggled in. I totally could not hide my utter joy. "Don't you know what this means?" I said as I watched Murray and Sean splashing around in the pool, and De yelling from the side, "Get out! You idiots!"

Buff Bobby looked at me, still horrified.

I clued him in. "It means Murray and De are back together. This is so dope!"

Then I turned to him and looked directly into his eyes. "This is a sign, Bobby."

"A sign?" He looked way doubtful.

"Tomorrow's going to be the bomb. Totally historic."

And then I did something way impetuous. I stood on my tiptoes, threw my arms around Bobby's neck, and kissed him.

Later I tried to find the exact right words to describe Bobby's reaction. I settled on surprised.

# Chapter 11

I don't know when I fell asleep, because when the alarm went off, it felt as though I hadn't slept at all. My stomach was doing a major butterfly concerto.

My hairstylist and my volumist showed up precisely at eight. I mean, what good is uber-stylish hair if it's flat? Then it was time to get into my ensemble. It's a good thing Lucy was there. I know I haven't added poundage, but I needed her to help me squeeze into my new shiny vinyl tangelo workout ensemble. It was way admirable how the sportswear company had done the skirt-to-shorts transformation. Even if it felt a little sticky.

I was sorry Daddy wasn't there. I wanted him to see how well his money had been spent. But Daddy wasn't due back until tomorrow night. So when I was ready, I went downstairs and pirouetted in front of Mom's portrait to show her my outfit.

"Wish me luck, Mom," I whispered, pressing two fingers to my mouth and sending the kiss Mom's way. Maybe I misinterpreted, but it seemed to me that Mom looked a little worried.

And okay, so maybe it wasn't the best sign when the chimes rang and Lucy opened the door to reveal . . . When did I invite Amber to come with me?

And what's she wearing? Whoops, my bad. When I was choosing workout ensembles, I hadn't envisioned Amber in them. And then to give her one in lime—what was I thinking? If she even has a color, it's grapefruit. When they're all tart and make your face scrunch up.

Amber added her own touches to my fashion statement. She totally exceeded the accessory limit with three gold necklaces, innumerable bangle bracelets, and an ankle chain. Worse, she punctured her bustier with an Elect Honest Amber button.

"Today's the big day!" Amber burbled rhetorically. Then, surveying the domed foyer, asked, "Where's Fred?"

"Who's Fred?" I asked, wondering if she could switch outfits with Tai.

"Fred, your father's helper. Isn't he coming with us to the Quad?"

"No. Like, why would you even think so?"

"We're not driving ourselves there?" Amber asked. "I mean, we're the stars. How would that look?"

The driver, a slug in flannel, materialized. Josh

looked startled when he saw me. "What are you wearing?" he asked.

"Just the bomb of all workout gear," I said, twirling around for full effect.

"I don't think I've ever seen—" Josh began.

"There's a lot you haven't seen, classroom-breath," I said. "Let's rock 'n' roll."

Bobby and his crew were already at the Quad when we arrived. I actually gasped when I saw him. The DKNY Tech tank I'd picked for him was white-hot. Paired with the form-fitting bike shorts, Bobby was a force of nature. I rushed up to him.

And then? I could not believe the same idiotic words came out of my mouth that Amber had uttered only moments earlier. But there I was, all "Today's the big day!"

Bobby grinned.

"You like the ensemble?" I asked. Okay, so I was fishing for a compliment.

"Well, uh, it looks great on you," he said hesitantly. "Some of my dancers aren't too wild about them, though."

"They *are* different," I acknowledged, "but we're making history here, on the exercise and the fashion front," I started to explain.

"Bobby! Bobby! Over here!" I didn't get to finish the thought, because one of the wired AD's was calling. Some tech matter screamed for Bobby's prompt attention.

At that very second, something screamed for mine, too.

Okay, so I had refused to take Amber at my door as a sign. But when Tai appeared at the Quad, I had to consider the possibility of some glitches in my plans.

Tai would have looked amazing. Tangerine was so her color. Only one vital accessory was missing—her left arm. It was in a cast, of the wrist to shoulder variety. The damaged appendage was secured close to her chest via an unsightly white sling.

I rushed up to her. "Tai, what happened?"

Her head hung in shame. Her spiraling curls covered her face. "I'm sorry, Cher, I didn't mean to spoil your video, but I don't think I can be in it. Not like this."

"Tai, you were fine last night. What happened?"

Tai looked way woeful. "It's Peabo, my training dog. He drooled all over the floor. You know, on the ceramic tiles at the bottom of the stairs."

I totally did not think I wanted to hear anymore. I was sure of it when Tai continued. "I was coming down the stairs, and just as I stepped onto the floor, I dunno, I went flying. I must've slipped in a pool of Peabo's drool."

I was way horrified. Tai lifted her arm away from her chest as far as she could. "It's broken in four places."

"Tai, I am so majorly sympathetic. Does it hurt?"

"Nah, not anymore. I can't feel nothin'," she said resignedly.

"Well, there's got to be a way for you to be in the video, even with that."

But Tai shook her head. "How can I swing my arms? How can I put them behind my head for the crunches? How can I lunge?"

In the end, I had to agree. Tai could be with us in

spirit, but teenage America was going to be denied her visuals.

I started toward Buff Bobby to break the Tai news, when I got distracted. De had arrived and was sashaying up to me.

"Girlfriend!" I tried hopefully. "I guess you're planning to change into your workout ensemble here?"

De was decked out in geometrics that might have been Versus. A bold plaid halter top and shorts-skirt slung low enough to reveal a waist chain with a heart on it. She pointed to it, gushing. "It's from Murray."

She had a headdress on, too. At least her sneakers were regulation Reeboks. But there was no citrus in sight.

De looked at me slyly. "I wasn't planning on changing, Cher. The outfits you got just don't make it for me."

I was buggin' big time. But after all we'd been through, I didn't want to get into a conflict with De. Besides, I wasn't sure if I felt disappointed or betrayed. Betrayed won.

"Maybe if you'd spared a few minutes of your precious empowerment time to shop with me, we could have come up with something that *does* work for you."

De just sniffed.

"You're going to clash with everyone, De!" I moaned.

"Hair and makeup everyone!" One of the assistant directors was rounding us up, pointing to a trailer parked by the side of the Quad.

I decided to deal with De's ridiculous fashion decision later. I stalked off toward the trailer to make sure Tony the makeup artist had arrived. Shawana and Shaniqua were already there. I was majorly relieved that De's minions hadn't copied her. At least they were in my outfits. And I had to admit, they totally looked like hotties in them.

When it was my turn, I let Tony do his magic on me and pranced out to meet Bobby. I was so ready to make workout history!

The places we were to stand in had been marked off. As I went to get into position, I surveyed our cast. I couldn't see what the dancers had to complain about. My fashion sense had done wonders for them. The outfits had totally turned mundane Monets into bodacious Bettys. Especially that long-limbed redhead from yesterday. Between my lime outfit and Tony's makeup, her skin looked way creamy, and her green eyes majorly dramatic.

I glanced over to the sidelines. Josh was leaning against a tree, his arms folded. I couldn't read the expression on his face, but I did notice, like again, how developed his triceps had gotten. Tai was plopped on a bench next to him, looking way forlorn.

A few teachers and random representatives of all our school's major cliques were there to witness history in the making. But what made my heart totally sing was seeing Fabianne. Because of her suggestion, a dream was coming true. Bobby's—and mine. I mean, so De and Tai hadn't contributed as much as I'd wanted them to. And Tai isn't exactly *in* the video. And De's in it, but in the wrong outfit. Still, all my t.b.'s were together, and together we were helping all of teenkind. Wake me when it gets better than this.

"Places, people!" Bullhorn Harry was up front, tapping his tiny foot.

When everyone was ready and in place, Harry commanded, "Action!" The music started, and we began our breathing warm-ups.

Soon Harry signaled that it was time to start my narration. I did. Except for the puzzled expression on the script supervisor's face, there was no reaction to my script revisions. After I recited like, the prologue, I introduced Bobby to the camera. He did a dazzling dental display and began to lead the way.

"And front, back, step together step, move it to the right, move it to the left, pull it up, and up!" Bobby intoned, with more enthusiasm than I'd ever heard. "Side to side, take a walk, to the right, dip it down, and left, and take a walk, dip it down, to the left. Stretch it out—"

"Cut!" Harry brutally interrupted our warm-ups. The sound engineer had signaled that he was hearing something definitely not on Jesse's soundtrack.

"What is that noise?" Harry demanded. "Let's take it without the music so we can smoke out that awful sound."

It didn't take long. The cacophony was courtesy of Amber. Her bracelets and bangles were crashing against each other every time she swung her arms. But instead of being properly embarrassed, Amber was way affronted when ordered to remove them. "They're heirlooms!" Amber whined. "If I take them off, they'll never be preserved on video."

"Okay, from the top, people," Harry ordered.

We started again. This time, we got through the breathing, my narration, and about halfway into the warm-ups when Harry yelled, "Cut!"

I looked around. What now?

"That boy in the back! What are you doing?" Harry pointed an angry, accusing finger at . . . I whirled around. Jesse! When had he arrived? Late, probably.

"Are we rolling?" Jesse asked stupidly. He looked directly into Camera Three and struck a pose. His legs were apart, one arm was crooked, the other pointing at the camera. Then he struck another pose. And another. Okay, so they were way cool, but Jesse wasn't exercising, he was vogueing!

"Young man!" Harry blared into the bullhorn. "Get with the program!"

"You wouldn't have a program, dude, if it wasn't for me. I got the music!" Jesse shouted, and then struck another pose.

Bobby scowled. At me. A spin control moment if ever there was one. I walked back to Jesse.

"Jess? Uh, could you pull it together? We're trying to get this shoot done. You know, the exercise tape?" I stage whispered in my most patient tone.

Jesse grabbed me and pulled me tight. He planted a big, messy kiss on my lips, and breathed, "For you, Cher, anything."

"You trashed my lipstick, you dunce!" I screamed, and ripped myself from his grip. Jesse just grinned. A big, stupid, grin. Then he vogued again.

"Bobby, hold up a sec," I pleaded, and dashed over to where Tony the makeup dude had set up by one of the fountains. Luckily, Tony expertly reapplied my lipstick quickly and I took my place next to Bobby. Harry signaled for the music to start again.

But we weren't two minutes into the routine when he yelled, "Cut!"

Someone's beeper had gone off. "Who's wearing a beeper?" Harry howled. Bobby turned around and growled, "We specifically said no beepers!"

This time the perp was Murray. "Sorry, man, but I had to get this call from the Tower distributor."

"No excuses! Ditch it!" Bobby was rounding the corner toward postal. He made it all the way there when Shaniqua sauntered off to a bench and picked up her cellular. "You! Put down that phone and get back in place!" he yelled.

Shaniqua's look was all, "You talkin' to *me?*" but what came out was only "I thought we were on a break."

"No breaks," Bobby snarled. "We've barely even started!"

I thought Bobby was acting way harsh, but I guessed it was to be expected. After all, he was totally on the spot. All that time we spent preparing, everything had led up to this day. And so far? Well, I didn't think it was going that badly. Only Bobby seemed to disagree.

Luckily, the next half hour went without major incident. We'd actually gotten all the way through the warm-ups and were ready for the cardio-funk aerobics. I thought we should capitalize on the momentum, but Harry was all, "Let's take a break and check the rushes." He and Bobby gathered by a small monitor to play back the tape and see how we looked so far. One of the AD's directed, "There's water and juice over by the fountain. I suggest everyone get some."

That was a good idea. I for one had started to sweat, and we hadn't even gotten to the aerobics yet. It was beginning to dawn on me why maybe vinyl outfits aren't normal workout gear. But they looked so dope!

A half hour later, we were ready to begin again. At Harry's signal, I began my introduction to the low-impact aerobics. I reintroduced Bobby. It hit me that he got, like, a lot of intros. Again, he flashed a major dental display at the camera and began to lead us.

"Step, step, step, step it in, pick your left leg up and out to the side, add some arms, in and out. Legs go back, arms go forward, push it, push it, cross the arms. Keep that heart rate up! Keep that energy up! Circle, and again, legs go back, arms go forward, add little swims. The knees come forward, pull it in, circle around. March it out, shake it out. Now shoulder roll! Now the body roll. Drop it down, roll it back up, a little bigger, elbows back—" Bobby was way into the rhythm, when Harry yelled, "Cut!"

This time, it was the operator on Camera Two who signaled a break in the action.

"What's up, Jimmy?" Harry walked over to his crew member.

"Take a look, Harry," the camera operator said, pointing into the lens. "See those girls in row two? They look like, I dunno, raccoons or something."

I flipped around. Oh, no. François Nars's expensive makeup had totally melted under the lights! The eyeliner, the eyeshadow, and the mascara had all, like, clumped together and started sliding off everyone's faces—on Bobby's dancers and my friends, too.

I ran to where I'd left my backpack and pulled out my compact. So far my makeup was okay, but my neck was riddled with red blotches. Don't let me break out now! All of teenage America will see it!

It took another forty-five minutes before everyone's makeup could be removed. Tony was way apologetic. As he packed up, he suggested that the dancers just do their own makeup, with anything they'd brought. I had another idea.

"De! We need you!" Whenever I was in a crisis of major makeup proportions, De always came to the rescue. And luckily, she was here now. Her words "I'll be there when you need me, Cher" flashed across the bottom of my mental screen. It took her about an hour and a half, but when De was done with all the dancing dudettes I wondered why I'd bothered with Nars and company in the first place. De was the all-time make-up maven.

Okay, so we'd wasted, like, a bunch of time, but now we were really ready. And we were furiously workin' it, too. That is, until we heard the scream. This time, Harry didn't even have to yell, "Cut." Everyone stopped and spun around toward the noise.

"My lens! My lens! I popped my lens! No one move!" Shawana was shrieking way frantically. She'd fallen to her hands and knees and was combing the grass for her contact lens. Then, we heard another loud voice.

"Whoa, baby, I'm here, I'll help you find it!" In his haste to come to the aid of his newly beloved, I guess Sean didn't see the thick electrical cable wires. As he tripped over them, he totally disengaged Camera One from its tripod. Sean was okay, though.

Which is more than I can say for Bobby, who was all "You klutz!" at Sean.

"How'd these get here?" Sean asked as he brushed himself off. "They weren't here during rehearsal."

"How would you know?" Buff Bobby scowled. "You barely showed up for rehearsal—and besides, numbskull, we didn't have cables because we weren't taping then." A little voice inside me said Bobby really shouldn't be hurling insults at Sean. Sean's just a kid.

Eventually, Shawana's errant contact lens was located, disinfected, and reinserted in her eye. We were now ready for some power funk high-impact aerobics. By far, the most punishing part of the regime. And as it turned out, we were totally punished.

But like, who could have predicted, just at the time we were elevating our heart rates that our shiny vinyl outfits would like, react to our perspiration by slipping and sliding off our bodies? The bustiers rode up, the shorts slid down. Resulting in major embarrassing moments.

Another previously unscheduled break was ordered so the dancers could be mopped up. I felt a tsunami of apprehension as Bobby stalked over to me, but I tried to keep my tone light and airy. I shrugged my shoulders and said, "What's next? Pestilence?"

I'm not quite sure Buff Bobby appreciated the joke, because he was all, "Let's not waste any more time." He decided that while the dancers were drying off, I "just do the rest of the narration." Harry explained that it could be looped in later, in the appropriate spots.

It was time for my close-up. In spite of my hives, I remembered that famous quote, like, "The show must go on." I did as told, took my place in front of Camera One, smiled brightly, and began.

"And now we're going to talk about exercises for all the significant moments of your life. Like at the Galleria. Though many see it solely as an important shopping experience, you could also view it as a huge exercise opportunity. I will now demonstrate the mall walk."

With that, I swung my hands at my sides and took giant steps forward. I looked side to side to simulate window shopping. As I did, I caught the stare of the script supervisor. I should have realized that her stomping over to Bobby was not a good sign.

I continued. "And then there's the Beverly Center. A way fabulous mall, housing the works of many important designers. But there are exercise opportunities everywhere you look. Since the Beverly Center is a vertical mall, you can think of it as your very own Stairmaster. Try jogging up the escalators instead of just standing there—"

I was just about to demonstrate, and then get to the part about how during algebra is a good time for butt crunches, and watching TV is totally the time to take your mat out and do the outer thigh eraser when I heard—

"STOP! Stop rolling!" Buff Bobby was waving his hands and shouting.

I looked at him. "What's the matter? Was the volume okay?"

Buff Bobby was like, advancing toward me, with a way menacing expression on his formerly gorgeous face, demanding, "What are you reading from? I told you to stick to the script!"

"I added important stuff," I said.

"You did what?" Bobby actually started to shout. At me!

From the corner of my eye, I saw a flash of Josh coming into camera range. But just then we were all stopped by a blood-curdling scream. Murray, Sean, Shawana, and De apparently had been off to the side, practicing a particularly complicated routine. When I turned toward the commotion, I saw Murray on the ground, grasping his leg and howling in pain.

"My leg! It's my hamstring! It's torn! Help!"

Right in the middle of Murray's excruciatingly high-pitched hysteria, Bobby snapped like uncooked pasta. "This is all your fault!" he yelled at me. "We'll never get this done! You and your spoiled brat friends. If you hadn't let them interfere—"

I couldn't believe what I was hearing. "My friends?" I said softly. My eyes started to brim as I looked at Buff Bobby. "The whole purpose was for my friends to be involved. To bring them all together and help humanity at the same time. To reunite. In our niche."

I turned to De, who was tending Murray.

"My man is hurt!" De shouted, rubbing his calf and cooing to him, "It's gonna be all right, baby." Then she blared, "Someone get ice! Call 411! I mean, 911!"

Bobby didn't even care that Murray was hurt. He

was still blasting me. "You're ruining my video! That's what I get for working with a bunch of immature, spoiled brats! I never should have let you do anything, Cher! Everything's wrong—the ridiculous outfits, your stupid friends. You blew it, Cher!"

I was crushingly bruised. I just stood there.

Josh was making his way toward us, ready to intercede, but suddenly, all I saw and heard was De. She'd jumped up and in a flash was right in between me and Bobby. De was furiously irate. And into major decibels.

"What'd I hear you say to my homegirl?" De growled, her eyes flashing. She was dangerously postal. "How dare you blame her! If it weren't for my friend, you'd be just another cheap hustler without a studio, or a client."

Bobby opened his mouth to retort, but he was no match for De. "My homegirl." No one does hissy fits better, or louder, than De. And she was on a major tear now. "You were supposed to be the adult in this situation. If you weren't so blinded by ambition and greed, you'd have seen this wasn't going to work. You led Cher on. She did all the work and you let her. You used her and now you're turning on her? I don't *think* so."

"I told you this wouldn't work with a stupid teenager!" And from this corner, another voice blasted into the fray. It was as high-pitched, hysterical, and as buggin' as De's. It was . . . the auburn-haired dancer?

"Marlene—" Buff Bobby began. "Sweetheart, baby."

*This* is Marlene? And he's calling her sweetheart?

Marlene was practically foaming at the mouth. "My father and his people put this whole deal together for you. Now he's gonna kill me! He warned me about falling in love with you! He told me you were a fast-talking loser!" Marlene started to kick Buff Bobby in his highly defined shins.

I felt the chunks rising in my throat. Bobby had a girlfriend all along? And one whose father turned out to be his people? Then it dawned on me. All those beeps that he didn't answer. Of course, it was her. Marlene was a benefactress all right. She was also a major hottie. Only right now she was hot to annihilate Bobby.

Bobby scowled at Marlene. "Wait a minute. We agreed on this. You and me together. We agreed I'd do this teenage video as a stepping stone, and then burst into the big time. Besides"—Bobby pointed at me—"you were the one who kept telling me to humor her. You were the one who said, 'Just go along with her, until the video gets done.'"

Bobby's voice was breaking—like my heart. "*You* were the one who even gave me that headband to give her."

Suddenly, another voice exploded above the din. Harry was on the bullhorn. Only this time he wasn't all "Places, people!" or "Action!" Or even "Cut."

He was yelling, "I quit! I've had it! I'm a professional here, and we can't work like this. It's over! I'm taking my crew and we're leaving. Pack it up, boys! I can't believe I wasted my time on this idiocy." Then, turning to Bobby, he said angrily, "You'll pay for my time on this!"

Bobby whirled around at Harry. He totally lost it.

"You quit? You can't quit! We have a contract! If you dare take one step out of here, I'll sue you."

At that, Harry went nuclear. "You'll sue me? Say that again? *You'll* sue *me?* Just try it, Mr. Super Trainer to the Stars. Yeah, right! I'll countersue so fast, you won't know what hit you." With that, Harry suddenly spun around and pointed at me. "In fact, I'll sue all of you, including your flaky little teenage partner here!"

I felt like I was in some alternate universe. I couldn't really be here. Not in a place where Bobby's in love with someone else. Where Bobby was just using me all along. A place where I'm getting sued by someone who thinks I'm flaky.

Suddenly, I heard Josh. He totally towered over Harry-the-postal-peanut. When he spoke, Josh's voice was clear and calm. But way forceful.

"Okay, that's enough. Don't talk to her that way. She's not to blame for this. If you've got a problem with him"—Josh pointed to Bobby—"deal with it. But don't bring Cher into this. And don't you dare threaten her."

Harry's face was furiously crimson. He lashed out at Josh, "Who are you? I'll see you all in court."

Josh remained calm. Daddy was right about Josh's flat head. Or something. He said to Harry, "I don't think so, man. This is between you and Van Hoosen. Don't imagine for one second you're involving Cher."

I still held out hope for Bobby. That he would, like, suddenly come to his senses, jump in, and side with Josh. But Josh didn't give him the chance. He blasted Bobby.

"And don't *you* think of dragging her into this,

either. When Mel signed the contract, we added a killer protection clause for Cher. Which you might not have noticed, being so focused on using her to promote yourself. I suggest you pack it up and take your problems elsewhere."

Josh turned to me. "Let's go, Cher. We're outta here."

"Uhm, does this mean there's no video?" Only Tai could ask that.

# Chapter 12

I'm not sure I fully appreciated the expression "crash and burn" before. But that's exactly what happened with my video project. Not only had it nose-dived to a fiery finale, the ashes were scattered everywhere. And I don't just mean the pile of vinyl workout ensembles the dancers had hurled at me as they packed up to leave the crash site. The Quad, that is.

Yet up until those very last seconds, I still held out hope. But when Harry and his team went AWOL and the blame-game heated up, I had to accept that it was really all over. No director, no crew, no money, and a trainer who turned out to be, well, not who I thought he was. In the end, all that could be heard above the hissy fits and harsh words were Murray's painful moans.

I was not unscathed. Leaving the scene, I was in a monster funk. With no video, my efforts to help all teenkind had come to naught.

Losing Daddy's money was way up there on the bummer scale, too. Along with his profit center from the video sales. But it wasn't just the material stuff that bugged me out. What if Daddy was disappointed in me? I so wanted him to see how responsible and entrepreneurial I could be. The words "You'll be investing in me, Daddy, and what could be better than that?" repeated on me like those greasy fries at Johnny Rockets. I would have to think of some positive spin by the time Daddy got home.

And then there was the reality check about my judgment in men. It felt like a swift kick in the abs. Washboard or not, it still hurt. Bobby had never been remotely interested in me romantically. He even thought I was spoiled! My friends saw right through Bobby and tried to warn me. How could I have been so clueless?

I might have stayed on the shame spiral longer, but self-flagellation is so not my style. So, after a cleansing shower, I put on sweats, called out for a double mochacinno from Caffeine Jones, and an extra cheese and pepperoni pizza from Spago. By the time Daddy called to see how the video had gone, I was feeling way better. Enough, anyway, to answer him with a vague, "Well, it was *eventful,* Daddy. I'll tell you all about it when you get home."

"I can't wait, Cher," Daddy had said. "By the way, I just want to tell you how proud I am that you held up your end of the deal. You didn't let the video take up all your time. Your schoolwork didn't suffer, and you helped me out with the Zinger depo, too. That's my girl."

I felt the double moccachino swirl nauseatingly in my gut and the pepperoni come up to choke me. The Zinger depo! I'd totally, majorly, intensely forgotten all about it. Worse, I wasn't sure where I'd left it.

Daddy would go from proud to postal in the time it takes a 'Vette to go from zero to eighty. Losing his money on the video thing was bad enough, but this was way more significant. What if my carelessness cost him the whole case?

I needed to pull it together. ASAP. I wished De were here. I wished Lucy were here. For the first time in my life, I wished my room wasn't so huge. I instituted an intense search-and-rescue mission. I was determined to find those files or trash my room trying. I checked every nook and cranny. But Zinger and his files were MIA.

I bent down to scour the floor of the drive-in closet, when I felt something. Unfortunately, not the files, but those weird vibes that were all déjà vu. Like I was not alone. I looked around, hoping against hope that Lucy had come in on her night off. But the form in the doorway wasn't Lucy's. It was in way better shape. And in lots more flannel.

Josh surveyed the chaos of my room and was all "What are you doing, Cher? Redecorating all by yourself?"

Under normal circumstances, I would have had a snappy comeback for Josh. But Josh had proved a stand-up dude, so it was ixnay on the verbal spars.

Besides I suddenly had the feeling that somehow, Josh already knew what I was doing—and why. "I've temporarily misplaced the Zinger files," I admitted woefully, and plopped down on the carpet.

Josh looked down at me weirdly. Like he cared, or something. "You can stop tearing your room apart," he said matter-of-factly. "I have them."

"You do? You stole them out of here?" I suddenly got energized and was halfway to nuclear. Josh took the files without telling me? How could he do that? I'd suffered horrendous mental anguish for the past like, forty-five minutes.

"Calm down, Cher," Josh said. "I didn't steal them. The files were mixed up with some pile of clothes you left on your floor. When Lucy was cleaning up *your* room"—Josh made it sound like *I* should be cleaning my room or something—"she found the files and gave them to me."

My rampant sigh of relief could be heard like, east of Rodeo. "Well, give them back. I need to finish highlighting before Daddy gets home."

"Relax, Cher. It's done."

"It is?" I was way dubious.

Josh clarified. "Truth is, you'd really done most of it yourself. I don't see how you found the time, but somehow you did. And it was all accurate. There were just a few pages left to do, so I finished them up. I gave the files to Mel just before he left. And just as he suspected, the dates matched and proved his point. Your father's about to win this case, Cher. And you helped him."

If Josh was like, anyone else, I would have jumped

up and thrown my arms around him in the biggest hug ever. But he was . . . Josh. So I just hung my head and looked up at him in the most contrite—and okay, cutest—manner possible. "Thanks, Josh. That was a major props you did. And with the video thing, too. I totally owe you," I said sincerely.

"Don't worry, Cher. I'll think of some way you can make it up to me." Josh smiled and his dimples showed.

He started to leave my room, when he suddenly turned around. "You hungry?" he inquired. I guess in all the mess, he hadn't seen the empty Spago's box. When I didn't answer right away, Josh said, "I haven't eaten all day. Want to go out for a bite?"

Food was the last thing on my mind, but if Josh wanted company, it was the least I could do.

"Just let me change, and I'll be ready in a flash," I said.

Josh shrugged his shoulders. "No need to change, Cher. We'll go to Jerry's Deli on Ventura. I'm sure you won't run into anyone you know there." Josh had a point. No one I know *would* be in the Valley on a Saturday night. The sweats stayed.

Later, over a double-decker corned beef sandwich for him, and a knish for me—well, with all the exercise I'd gotten lately, I was sure this wouldn't hurt—Josh went off on this how-much-he-worships-Daddy tangent.

"Mel is a brilliant attorney—and a compassionate human being. Two qualities I thought were mutually exclusive in a lawyer. I didn't appreciate Mel that much when I lived here. But now I see him from a different perspective. Less as a stepfather, and more as . . . I don't know . . . maybe even a mentor."

Josh was polishing off a sour pickle when he grinned and finished, "If I'm lucky, that is."

"So you, like, want to follow in Daddy's footprints and be a litigator?" I asked.

"I haven't got it figured out yet. But I have a while before I have to make a career commitment," Josh answered thoughtfully. Then he said, "What about you, Cher? Ever think of going the attorney route, like your father?"

I was way surprised Josh would say that. His opinion of my intellect hadn't ever been that high. And after the video debacle today, I couldn't imagine it had risen significantly.

I don't think I was actually flirting when I answered coyly, "Do you really think I have what it takes to be an attorney, Josh?"

Josh took a deep breath and said quietly, "I don't know, Cher. But in a lot of ways, you remind me of Mel."

"Not even!" I said passionately, "How could I remind you of anything but that superficial twinkie brain you always say I am? Especially after what happened today."

Josh put his sandwich down and leaned back in the booth. He folded his arms and looked at me way intently. "Okay, so the workout tape fell through, but from what I've observed, I don't think you have anything to apologize for. In fact, I think you should be proud."

I looked at what was left of Josh's sandwich for signs of tampering. Had he just eaten some personality-changing magic meat? Why was he all, like, on my side all of a sudden?

Josh continued. "Look at what you accomplished. You helped design the video, you learned all the routines, you arranged for the music, dressed everyone, and involved all your friends. All without missing a beat at school and helping Mel with the deposition . . . mostly."

There was no sign of sarcasm in Josh's soft voice. He was totally 'tudeless, as he finished, "That's a lot to accomplish, Cher."

"Well, I guess I am Mel's daughter," I said, giving him a major lopsided grin.

Josh continued. "You know, if anyone should be feeling lousy today, it isn't you. It's that Buff Bobby jerk. He's the one who screwed up. If he wasn't so into becoming a star, he might have had this thing better organized. You might even have actually pulled it off."

"You really think so?" I asked as we walked out to the car.

"I do. I mean, I admit at first I thought the whole thing was silly. But Mel saw its potential. Your father didn't invest only because you wanted him to, he believed it was a viable idea. One that could have been profitable. Mel believes in you, Cher. He felt that if any teenager could make this a success, it was his daughter."

"Daddy told you that?"

"He didn't have to, Cher."

* * *

On Sunday I decided to brighten up the lives of the injured with personal visits and gift baskets. I started at Tai's house. She was hugely psyched to see me. "It's so cool that you're here, Cher. I kinda made a big decision about Peabo, and I wanna share it with you."

The drooling dog, who had tried to nip me when I came through the door, wasn't the most stimulating topic, but I was all "I'm here for you, Tai. Tell."

She sucked in her breath and said, "Okay. Here it is. I'm giving him up."

"You mean, to the blind person?" I asked.

"No, Peabo isn't ready for that. I didn't do a good job preparing him—for his life's work, I mean." Tai sounded woeful.

"Tscha! Tai, how could you say that? I agree that maybe Peabo isn't ready to lead the blind, but maybe you just got— I don't know, can dogs be lemons?"

"No, Peabo's not a lemon," Tai said in that baby voice she used with the dog. She leaned over to stroke him affectionately with her one working arm. "It's just, I dunno, I guess I'm not cut out for this stuff."

"I don't know about that, but I do know this, Tai. Your motives were majorly pure. And you've got to give yourself snaps for the total dedication you brought to this project. I mean, all the hours you spent working with him." I looked over. Peabo had drooled on the carpet. I took a quick step back and looked away.

"That's another thing, Cher. In the last few weeks, I started to feel, like, overwhelmed with all the time I had to spend with him. I missed being with you and our t.b.'s."

Before I could like, give Tai a hug, she continued resolutely. "So tomorrow Peabo's going to his new family. A family with a lot more time—and patience."

"I have an idea, Tai," I said. "Since we're both clearing our calendars, how about we pencil in a study date for next week? Maybe if you bring up your grades, you won't have to worry about transcript enhancers and stuff."

Tai's eyes twinkled when she answered, "Only if we can do a few laps around the Galleria afterward." Our high five was way limper and more meaningful than ever before.

My visit with Tai had gone righteously. On to my next patient. While I totally shared Murray's pain, I hoped he was getting over it—in both the physical and psychic senses. Murray's distribution deals had snapped like his hamstring. I was hugely relieved when Murray hobbled to the door and answered it himself with a broad, braces-revealing smile and a hug.

"Yo, Cher, wussup? You comin' to pay respects to the injured?"

I gave Murray the gift basket and acknowledged that I'd come to see how he was doing. But Murray was all "I only got myself to blame. If I showed up at more rehearsals, I could've been more limber and all."

"So you're really okay? Even about Blockbuster and your distribution deals?" I asked hopefully.

Murray shrugged his shoulders. "What's not to be okay about? There's nothing to distribute. Anyway, my father called up Blockbuster and explained it was some natural disaster, like a random act of God, as to why we can't deliver. There was somethin' about it in the agreements. I guess I got a lot to learn about the business world."

"So then you're not, like, mad at me or anything?" I confirmed.

"You kiddin'? Until my leg heals, I get out of PE. Plus, I'm back with De. Life is good, Cher, and it's all thanks to you! Besides," Murray added playfully, "I might make some money on this whole thing yet."

I gave him a quizzical stare.

"Yeah, I'm gonna get my hands on the footage we did shoot and mail it in to *America's Funniest Home Videos.* We got that grand prize in the bag!"

# Chapter 13

I was watching *Lois & Clark: The New Adventures of Superman* when I heard Daddy's limo pull into the driveway. Just as Clark was about to give Lois a passionate kiss, I clicked it off. So much for fantasy. My personal reality was just coming through the door. I had to tell Daddy the truth, all of it. ASAP. Daddy didn't suffer procrastinators gladly. Especially if they were his daughter, who was about to find out just how burnt toast could feel.

I slunk down the stairs just as Daddy entered the marble foyer, and gave him my best welcome home hug. In spite of what I knew was about to transpire, it felt good having Daddy home. He didn't, like, interrogate me or anything. At least not right away.

"How was your trip, Daddy?"

"It was good, we won. But it's better to be home." Daddy looked tired.

"Are you hungry? I can make you some cocoa and, like, a sandwich."

I guess that must've tipped off Daddy. "Cocoa? A sandwich? Not some seaweed juice and a rice cake?" Daddy's eyebrows knitted dangerously and he perked up. He motioned for us to go into his office. "Sit down, Cher," he said, "and tell me what happened. All of it. Not just what you think I need to know."

I had no choice. I told him how like, in spite of rampantly conscientious preparations, everything had gotten out of control. About the slippery ensembles, the melted makeup, Amber's jewelry, Shawana's popped lens, Jesse's vogueing, Murray's hamstring, Harry walking out in a huff . . .

I was out of breath by the time I finished recounting the whole sad sorry saga. Daddy didn't go postal right away. He was all calm when he asked, "And what was Josh's role in all this?"

"Josh?" I was surprised at that being Daddy's first reaction. But I answered, "He was like, mature and all. He kind of intervened." And then I realized exactly what Josh's role had been. "He did what you would have done, Daddy. He was level-headed and calm. He enlightened Harry and Buff Bobby about the terms of the contract, that killer protection clause and all. And then he told them both where they could go."

Daddy nodded. "Good."

I looked at Daddy. "I'm sorry I lost your money. And I'm sorry if I disappointed you." In a tiny whisper, I added, "Are you mad, Daddy?"

Silently, I counted to ten. That's usually how long it takes Daddy to simmer up to major boiling. But instead of going nuclear, Daddy gave me a major paternal gaze. Then he put his arm around me, and drew me to his chest. I noticed how wrinkled his shirt had gotten and made a mental note to call the dry cleaners tomorrow.

Then Daddy said, "No, Cher, I'm not mad."

"Not even about the money?" I sniffled.

"Nah, that's the least of it. It's a write-off. And we'll need one, after winning the Zinger case, to which I might add, Cher, you contributed."

I don't know what made me fall into full confession mode, but when Daddy complimented me on Zinger, I realized there was some info left unspilled. "About the depo, Daddy?"

Daddy arched his eyebrows.

"Well, I did do it, like you asked. But I didn't exactly, completely, totally finish, like all of it."

Daddy looked puzzled. "Then who did? When Josh gave it to me—"

The way I looked up at Daddy gave him the answer.

"Well, I hope you learned something from all this, Cher," Daddy finally said. He had his faux-gruff voice back. Which is when I knew he really wasn't mad after all.

"Of course I did, Daddy. Shiny vinyls and work-outs just don't mix."

"Not that! I mean, I hope you learned something about friendship. The video was one thing, but you didn't have to go to such lengths to get your friends back. Your friends never left, Cher. No one who truly cares about you ever would."

That night, I fell into the deepest, most restful sleep I'd had in months.

The next morning I woke to the most joyful noise in all of teendom: the ringing of my phone. Which could only mean one thing—I'd left the video scene with my popularity still intact. Only the voice on the other end wasn't a random admirer or an important t.b. It was Amber.

"I'm calling to remind you about today's big debate, Cher. It's *très* important, the last one before the election. Just me against Brian. And may I remind you, you missed all the others."

My call-waiting was beeping, so I cut her off with a, "Be cazh, Amber. I'll be there," and clicked off. Tai was on the line with an emergency fashion question. "Should I wear the camisole top or the jersey T with the Nicole Miller mini?" As I gave her my recommendation, I could feel myself starting to glow with contentment. Everything really was getting back to normal. When the phone rang again, it was De. "Let's do the après-school thing. Meet in the Quad after last period?"

I was totally humming as I bounced down the stairs and swung into the kitchen. Lucy was scrambling up some eggs. I hoped they weren't for Daddy, since she hadn't separated the yolks.

"Hey, Luce, zup?"

"Good morning, Cher. How did your video go?"

I flashed back to that morning when Lucy was all

struggling with *Buns of Steel.* I felt a stab of guilt that I'd totally ignored Lucy's physical fitness. I had promised to help her, too.

"Not so well, Luce," I admitted, "but in my research, I did find something you might like." I dashed into the Great Room and pulled out all the Richard Simmons videos. Okay, so they're not exactly for housekeepers, but they do feature the most glutally diverse dancers in the entire spectrum of workout videos. Lucy would fit right in.

I wasn't sure what the general tenor would be among the school population. I knew that by homeroom, word about the video would have spread like those chemicals off the Exxon *Valdez.* But as it turned out, few generics said anything, let alone anything negative. My video was totally yesterday's sound bite. The only vestige of video madness was Jesse—formerly known as Jesse the prince of free music, now just Jesse the annoying jerk.

He was singing at the top of his lungs. "Cher-y, Cher-y, bay-yay-bee." I sort of recognized the tune from an old record in Daddy's vinyl collection by some rockers-with-walkers called the Four Seasons.

"Where's my video vixen speeding off to?" Jesse said smarmily, wrapping himself around me.

"Jesse? I have a news flash for you. I'm not your anything." I freed myself from his embrace but not of his idiocy.

"But I got you, babe. You and me. We're a team, making beautiful music together."

As I brushed past Jesse, I tossed him a reality dart.

"Your music rules, Jesse, but I've escaped your kingdom." By the expression on his face, I could tell I'd missed the bullseye. Jesse—and his ego—both winked at me.

Thanks to the sidebar with Jesse, I was late for Amber's debate. Which as it turned out, was something to be grateful for. First, there was Amber's ensemble. For her Great Debate, she'd chosen an Anna Molinari shiny green patina pantsuit. Okay, so I know, like, how shiny is in. And how it screams, "Look at me." Only Amber's was just screaming.

Worse, Amber was getting clobbered, big time, by Brian. Although, I have to admit, visually, Brian matched Amber in no-appeal. He'd clearly gone overboard with the hair gel, and I'm not sure what impact he thought a nerd in a leather jacket would have. My best guess? He was going for Jimmy Dean the actor but came off all Jimmy Dean the sausage. Still, oratorically speaking, he sizzled. Amber fizzled.

All that time Amber spent making posters, giving passionate support-group speeches, and doing the video, Brian developed a strategy. Instead of talking RAM and megahertz, Brian was all, "And if I win, my parents will donate new vending machines with Arizona Iced Tea, Snapple, cappuccinos, double lattes, and Chee-tos. And you can use your credit card to access any of it."

I knew it before the room exploded in applause. In the battle of easy-access, upscale junk food vs. something so ethereal as credits for support groups, you had to go with the digestive system. Amber was going down fast. Which even she seemed to grasp. She went for one last desperate attempt, imploring her audience, "Don't be so short-sighted! My platform will serve you better in the long run! His will only give you zits!" But it was way over. Ambu-loser was down for the count.

Amber glumly slithered down from the stage. I went up to her. "Forget the election, Amber. Focus on tomorrow. Focus on the positive."

She looked at me doubtfully.

Quickly, I tried to come up with something that was positive. The best I could do was "There'll always be Fred."

Amber's shiny patina pants suit seemed to have affected her complexion. She looked green. "You think so?" she said unconvinced.

"Tscha, Amber. I have it on good authority"—of course, I had it on no such thing—"that he'll be back working with my father on the next case. And if you want to come and visit—" I tried to stop myself, but some powerful, driving force made me continue. "And I think Fred likes you."

Okay, so that might not have been accurate. Not yet. But maybe if I do a makeover on both of them, well, as someone once said to me, who knows what might develop?

I knew my work was done when Amber began to prattle about how her talents were so wasted on the sophomore class, and so much better appreciated by a law student like—I was Audi before she tacked the *d* on Fred.

De was waiting for me in the Quad. She was wearing something from her pre-*Exhale* days, a bare-with-flair look involving a silk denim halter, matching pants, and jacket with gold piping. Instantly identifiable as Richard Tyler. I gave her an admiring once-over, ignoring the fact that I don't think Richard envisioned belly beads with the look.

De was all, "Where to, girlfriend? CPK's?"

I had a better idea. "Let's push the trend envelope and try something radically different." I was thinking, the Trat. I'm so over Buff Bobby, but why throw out the baby with the bathwater? Or something.

De's once-over confirmed her approval of the Trat. And as long as the service was up to her standards, this could totally become a new Cher-and-De-discovered-it-first hangout.

But a weird feeling came over me when we were seated. For the first time in all our friendship, I wasn't sure what to say to De. So much had happened between us. And I still wasn't exactly sure where she was, on her journey and all? I mean, De had been the most righteous t.b. ever at the video shoot. She'd totally stood up for me and blasted Buff Bobby. If I put that together with today's outfit, did that mean we were like, back?

As De ordered her drink, "Make sure the ice is made from mineral water," she sounded so much like her old self, it gave me the courage to ask her.

"So, De, zup with your journey? Did you like, find your inner African-American princess? Did you find yourself?"

De went into major thoughtful. "I discovered a lot, Cher. For one thing, I never lost myself. It was there all along."

I was confused and it showed. De explained, "I did learn about my heritage, Cher. And I'm proud of it. All sides of it. I'm unique."

"Well, duh, girlfriend, I could have told you that!"

"And I'm proud of my uniqueness," De continued. "I celebrate it. But it's not just my genetic makeup that sets me apart, it's my sense of independence. When I thought about what you said about me and Murray, I realized you were right, Cher."

"Then it wasn't Murray joining the football team that made you realize how much you loved him?"

De laughed. A major deep, throaty laugh. "The football team! My jellyfish man? I don't think so! It was you who made me realize how much I love Murray. Not your see-through scheme to make me all concerned about him, either."

De knew about my scheme?

"Tscha, Cher! It was what you said that day in the girl's room. When I thought it over, I realized you were right about me and Murray. He is my soulmate, we do belong together. I never used him to define me. I mean, maybe some women still think they need a man to be all that, but not me. You never did, either, Cher. I guess when it comes to relationships, you can't generalize."

De was laying some major heavies on me. And it felt so good. Softly, I said, "You were right all along about me and Buff Bobby. I mean, it wasn't a total loss—I did get washboard abs out of it, and they're such a fashion statement right now. But Bobby was never interested in me, not past the video anyway. He was only using me, like you said. But I didn't listen to you."

At that second, De wasn't listening to me. Her attention had been sharply diverted. She pointed to a table in the corner. "Speaking of the himbo . . ."

Buff Bobby! And he's, uh, not alone. But that's not Marlene. He's with . . . I craned my neck . . . Fabianne? De and I tried to eavesdrop. When we heard the words "massage video," we started to laugh and went back to our soul-baring conversation.

"You know what I just realized, De?" I said. "Buff Bobby may have been using me, but in a sense, we were all using other people. I mean, I was totally using Jesse just for the free music."

De giggled. "There's a difference there. You can't hurt Jesse. Besides, he deserves whatever's flung his way."

I continued, "And come to think of it, even though, like, Tai's motives were totally pure, she was kind of using the dog to advance her own transcript."

And then it hit me. In a sense, Ambu-loser was the only non-user. She was, after all, honest. Isn't it ironic? I turned back to De. "So now that you and Murray are back, do you still feel empowered and stuff?"

De got all serious. "One thing empowerment comes from is friendship, Cher. Knowing you have someone who will always be there for you, no matter what duh-head mistakes you make."

We both grinned. "That's empowerment."

"You were always there for me, De, even when I thought you weren't."

"I never meant to cut you off, Cher. That's why I really agreed to do the video with you. I didn't trust Buff Bobby as far as I could throw the sucker, but I could see how much it meant to you. That's the real reason I said I'd do it."

"So it had nothing to do with my inviting Shaniqua, Shawana, and Essence into it?" I asked.

"Okay, that *was* important," she admitted. "I mean, they are my friends. We're still cool, but—" De paused.

"But what?" I asked.

"Nothing, Cher. They're just not you. That's what."

Before I could like, tear up, De said something else. "You know the most significant thing I learned on my journey?"

I waited.

"Something else about friendship. The only color that matters is blue—as in true."

"Well, I learned something about friendship, too," I quipped. "It's a famous poem. 'Friends are the people who let you be yourself—and never let you forget it.' "

De's eyebrows arched. "Hey—that's no poem, that's a line from *Exhale*."

I nodded. "Totally, sister."

And then we reached across the table and hugged.

# About the Author

Randi Reisfeld is the author of *Clueless: An American Betty in Paris* and the best-selling *The Kerrigan Courage: Nancy's Story* (Ballantine, 1994), as well as over a dozen books about young celebrities. Also available from Archway Paperbacks is the exciting biography *Joey Lawrence.* She has also written *Meet the Stars of Melrose Place* and *So You Want to Be a Star!: A Teenager's Guide to Breaking into Showbiz.* Her *The Stars of Beverly Hills, 90210: Their Lives & Loves* has been translated into a dozen foreign languages, as has *The Official Baywatch Fact File.* Books for adults include *The Bar/Bat Mitzvah Survival Guide* and *When No Means No: A Guide to Sexual Harassment,* which she co-authored. Her most recent book is *This Is the Sound: Today's Top Alternative Bands* (Aladdin, 1996).

As editorial director of *16* magazine, Ms. Reisfeld has interviewed and written about the most popular stars of television, movies, and rock 'n' roll. Her articles have appeared in *The New York Times, Scholastic, First for Women,* and *Women's World Magazine.* Additionally, she writes a celebrity column for *Chatterbox,* a BBC publication in Great Britain.